Ready o1

Will we ev

MW01688611

President George Crush

(pronounced "Croosh")

Could his people have been selling CRACK COCAINE to the Bloods and Crips in South Central LA?

What about a Los Angeles Narcotics Detective who claims to be one of SEVERAL EYEWITNESSES?

Why was a lawsuit against the Government THROWN OUT OF COURT before they even presented their first witness?

How could a GOVERNMENT LIE to their own citizens?

Pues, maybe some of us half know it for a while...

"Now that I'm awake..."

武士道

BuShiDo
The Movie
(based on true story)

Bernardo Gonzolez

PARKING VOUCHER:

"All the similarities to Peoples (past, present, and future) ain't necessarily so. It's just your imaginations, playing tricks on you. Baby, don't even look like you. My Lawyer says so.....

....My Manager backs that up.

- Chuchi

Translation (Spanglish to English): This is a work of fiction. All of the characters and events protrayed in this work are either fictitious or are used fictitiously.

BUSHIDO

A MindLess Productions Moving Picture
Published by MindLess Publications

ISBN: 978-0-9800493-0-5

Library of Congress Catalog Number: 2007938511

First Edition November 2007

Printed in the USA

You just don't know who's going to call DJ Cassius Timmons:

RAMON "SPEEDY" GONZALEZ
(speaking real fast)
Eh! Am I on the radio?! This is Ramon. Is this where you asking all the any kinds of crazy retarded questions?

PACO "SLOW-POKE" RODRIGUEZ
Tell 'em Speedy, let 'em know!

DJ
Alright, so you got one question you want answered, right? And that one question is?

RAMON "SPEEDY" GONZALEZ
Is you President of the United States George W. Crush and his super-Protestant #1 lady - Is they a part of a mafioso type Drug Dealing family that been pushing drugs onto little kids since all the way back to the 1950's -
(looks over at Slo-Poke, who looks back at him with a HUGE smile spreading over both their faces)

SPEEDY AND SLO-POKE TOGETHER
- OR WHAT?!!!!!!

WHOLE BIKE GANG
OR WHAT?!!!!! OR WHAT, OR WHAT, OR WHAT?!!!!!!!!!
(chorus picks up again stronger than before) OR WHAT?!!!!!
OR WHAT?!!!!! OR WHAT, OR WHAT, OR WHAT?!!!!!!!!

SPEEDY
This telephone gonna self-destruct in just a coupla seconds, j'OK?

DJ
WHAT?!!!!

SLO-POKE
DALE, CABRON!!!!!

WHOLE BIKE GANG
SI!!!! VAYA!!!!! DALE!

SPEEDY
(pulling big silver revolver)
Stan' back!!!!! (drops receiver) !Toma!!!!! (shoots payphone until coins spill out of coin slot)

SOUND OF DIALTONE

#3
Line's dead, Cassius.

DJ
All right that's fine. Good-bye!
(hangs up on call) (to himself:)
Did Crush deal drugs?
What in God's name do we do with this?

"...Tiny purple fishes

... run laughing through your fingers."

This is dedicated to Robert "Gismo" Rodriguez who showed me that you don't know what you're capable of - every day you're alive you could change anything. People don't believe...

...and to my father Manuel Ricardo José Blanco-González who gave me the tools of the trade and showed me that sometimes staying alive only just one more day - even under great pain and stress - might be just exactly what God is asking of you... who showed me just how strong some one's heart and lungs can be...

And to Ralph Ellison - the greatest - who told me to be my own father. I listened to you more than anyone.

Rest in Peace.

Bushido Introduction

There were necessities.
The bait on the jook.
Blue Fish
Blue water
Deep Blue
He was crazy.
Crazy for looking directly at the sun.
Crazy-er still he hasn't blind. He was looking at the SUN like so.
And so.
There might be RE-percussions
At the moment he didn't care anymore. Repercussions didn't rate.
He was looking at the SUN.
The real SUN.
Not the crazy fake cut-out that priests and politicians
and doctors use as a mask for ritual killings and mass hallucinations…
There was too much Percussion going on for him to concern himself with Re-Percussions.
It was raining -
Hard.
Blue Black water on a sea of discarded crack pipes…
And on the horizon -
clearly visible → → cause he was flying
→ → A TSUNAMI → → →
several deep BLACK BLUE MEXICAN
TIDAL WAVES OF HEROIN…

Re-Percussions were for suckers who couldn't hear straight.
And the real SUN was warming his body.
Filling it with light
Just like so many other goats scattered on the grassy hills and mountains.

The light was traveling deep to his heart -surrounding it
- warming him to the core. It was traveling with him like
Dolphins racing around his blood vessels. They loved him.
No question.
He followed that light through traffic lights - past stop signs,
all the written shit posted to explain what you were seeing.
He followed it through crowds of angry people. He read other
signs with growing fluency…
He was blind to the explanations. He was seeing the rawness.
He was flying like a crow flies.
Illiterate by choice
Retarded like a spark

Out of sight

10° BTDC

Before Top Dead Center

He was just slightly ahead
of full compression

Ask your mechanic.

He wasn't a Crow
Or a Sioux
Or a Cherokee   line of sight

He was a flying Pollock Bastard
Who spoke the language
And ignored the Sin Tax

belief

Flying involves confidence
He was good enough at it to fly through a sewer pipe.
Flying blind
Because a sewer pipe has got no light
And then
Underground.

a miracle.

He flew through the walls of the sewer pipe to a steel tower - architects trapped drafting new sickness sewers - sealed underground festering rivers that had nothing to do with aquifers leading to beautiful clean spring waters, filtered through rock sand charcoal pumped upwards out of mountain tops… He flew blind to the known fact that Pollacks cannot fly. Nowitzki wasn't Polish

No way.

He flew to the steel towers of the architects ordering the waters of the world to be orderly.
Not a drop.
All in pipes
Bound for somewhere.
Bound in captivity
Running around mazes of captivity
Like a Pollack flying through sewers of death, holding his breath, looking to re-connect to the way a crow flies over a smokestack - or a Cherokee runs out a convenience store.

A microscopic dolphin jumps out the walls of an artery - like tai chi radio does - and back in again.

A fellow traveler.

GOD

- In a coffee shop. Losing sight of the fact that I'm supposed to be working - following this to lose that sign.

And so.

Characters:

The DJ (CASSIUS TIMMONS) - an LA Talk Radio DJ

#3 - the DJ's Radio Co-host

KWAME - another of the DJ's Radio Co-hosts

POPPA ZEE - A man in Timmon's old neighborhood who shines shoes

MICHAEL RUPPERT - Former LAPD Narcotics Officer

ERNESTO - A College Student from El Salvador

SALVADOR - A Baseball Player/Coach from El Salvador

PRESIDENT GEORGE CRUSH (Pronounced "Croosh") - President of the United States

SENATOR JOHN QUERY (of Massachusetts) - former Democratic Presidential Candidate who opposed Crush in the last election

LT. COL. OLIVER NORTH - The President's #1 man in the NSC during Iran-Contra

FAWN HALL - Oliver North's Secretary who aided in the destruction of documents

THE PROFESSOR - A College Professor teaching a class on the "Theory and Practice of the Modern Drug Industry"

CASSANDRA TIMMONS - Cassius Jr.'s younger sister, who dies of a heroin overdose at age 16

CHRISTIC INSTITUTE - Attorneys that brought a case against the US Government

WASHINGTON SENATORS BASEBALL TEAM - the Team Salvador works for as a 3rd base coach

OPENING SEQUENCE:

Intro

· Andean Swordsman – Quechua music

· The Opium War – written on screen with scenes from Chinese docks.

· Martin Luther King – A hypertension of words and an anemia of deeds.

· George Bush, Sr.: "The War on Drugs."

· stock footage: The aerial bombing of El Salvador during the War on Drugs.

· George McGovern – From book "All the President's Men" (Chap 4, p.74) get speech or quote on TV "This (Watergate) Investigation is a White Wash…What is involved here is not only the political life of this nation, but the very morality of our leaders at a time when the United States desperately needs to revitalize its moral standards. And that is why I shall pursue this case the length and breadth of this land." Sunday, Sept. 16th, 1972.

INT. means "Interior"

EXT means "OUTSIDE"

i.C.U. means i CLOSE UP

Important Noticero:

This book is a **MOVIE**

Not a novel

You have to read into it with

3-d glasses

(COME INCLUDED WITH YOU BASIC PACKAGE)

EXT. - ANDEAN MOUNTAINS - DAY
MUSIC: At first a low pitched Japanese bamboo flute plays in time with a man dressed in traditional clothing but practicing moves with a Japanese Sword; the Japanese flute slowly blends into the Grupo Aymara – Andean traditional Native music, bamboo flutes, bomba drums, music with roots older than recorded history, this particular piece has a deep bass rhythm that advances like waves pounding the shore. It carries with it the force of hundreds and thousands of years of generations moving over the mountains, carving steps in the stone and wearing those steps down just like water carving out a canyon, we move past the swordsman over the mountains to people working in the coca fields swinging machetes to the rhythm of the music, loading the bags of leaves onto trucks, the trucks going to the "distillery", then to the boats and then the boats heading out to sea, through the Panama Canal, and then on to Miami... this section is like Koyaanisqatsi in feel.

CREDITS ROLL

MUSIC: The sequence continues but the music changes drastically. Now it has radio static and we cut back and forth to sound bytes and then music – bits of speeches from The War on Drugs – crowds cheering – various drug related songs (White Lines, Freddies Dead) This section feels more like Enemy of the State (Will Smith, Gene Hackman)

Act I: Can I Ask the Question?

ESTABLISH SALVADOR "You hit the Plane!"

EXT. BASEBALL FIELD – EL SALVADOR – DAY

A dusty baseball field with a chainlink fence on one side and a barnyard on the other marking left and right field with a broken down tractor right in the middle of center. 15 YR. OLD SALVADOR is at the plate, getting ready for the pitch.

SALVADOR
Dale, ya! (Throw it already!)

A big CARGO PLANE is flying in back of the pitcher as the pitch comes and Salvador tears the cover off the ball, all the KIDS' heads track the ball as it sails up over them. Close up of the plane's side as the ball miraculously hits one of the engines.

KID #1
You hitting the Plane! You hitting the Plane!
All the kids run around yelling and screaming "You hitting the Plane!" The planes engines falter in the background as it looks and sounds like the plane might crash, but then it rights itself and heads off screen.

CUT TO:

EXT - WASHINGTON, DC, WHITE HOUSE – NIGHT

CUT TO:

INT - OLIVER NORTH'S OFFICE IN NATIONAL SECURITY COUNCIL – NIGHT

SUBTITLE: "Lt. Colonel Oliver North's Office - Washington, D.C. - 1982"

Subtitle: "A DRAMATIZATION" appears in top right corner of screen and stays there throughout all scenes involving Oliver North and Fawn Hall.

MUSIC: Somber and Foreboding Cello music - dark tones

As the camera pans in towards North's cluttered desk, a map of Central America appears superimposed like an onion skin overhead projection on the screen. It is the map North is studying. He scribbles notes and arrows on the map with a pencil that appear on the onion skin map - numbers, troop movements, cash amounts. Boxed text with arrows appear on the onion skin map pointing to countries and features: "Columbia", "Panama", "Costa Rica" "John Hull's Ranch", (the projected map moves North), "El Salvador", "Ilopango Airport", "Honduras", "Nicaragua" (the map enlarges to highlight Nicaragua)"Managua", "Harbour Entrance" Lines and Circles are drawn on the map: "FDN." "Calero" "Saudi Arabia - Bandar - $1 million/month"

Numbers from a checking account scroll down the screen, headed by caption "TRANSFER FUNDS"
His eyes grow heavy. He looks over at two pictures on his desk. One - wife and kids at a "Company" picnic. Then he looks at the other - Fawn Hall - his secretary - a close-up. His eyes/the camera zooms in: Blond hair, blue eyes, just a bit of cleavage Close up shot of his eyes drooping. It's late, and he's tired. Back to photo of Fawn Hall. Camera goes out of focus and back in again. And the music starts - so soft it's almost imperceptible but unmistakable: The Beach Boys - I Wish They All Could Be California Girls - just the intro - the sing song "Dee-da Dee-da, Dee-da, Dee-da"

PHONE RINGS SHARPLY;

NORTH
Hello? Yes? (sharp tones of nagging on other line) Oh, yeah, honey, no I'm leaving now. Just had to get these numbers together - big day tomorrow. Coffee? No problem.

CUT TO --> SUDDEN CLOSE UP OF HIS LIPS AS HE CONTINUES HIS THOUGHT SAYING:

- Is a kilo enough? (sharp sudden drum roll sound that cuts off instantly)

CUT TO :

MRS. NORTH
What did you just say?

NORTH
(internal voice in head:) “Did I say that?”
I meant a pound (fumbling) a pound - how about some ice cream, too. Does that sound good?

MRS. NORTH
(sarcastically)
Yeah, how about a kilo of ice cream.

NORTH
(forced) Yes. - Yes. - Vanilla sounds good. Look - I - I gotta go. I'll be home before you know it. Love you, dear –

CUT:

ESTABLISH DJ – Radio station

INT. - RADIO STATION HALL WAY – DAY

Weaving through the crowded hallway, saying a quick “hi” to the people he brushes past, a RADIO DJ heads into the soundproof just as the SPORTSCASTER is finishing up

SPORTSCASTER
The Lakers will be facing Chicago tonight for the start of a 4 game series. That kicks off at 7:30 tonight, and that's it in sports (looking over as DJ sits down)

The DJ slides into his chair, slipping his headphones on, while his SIDEKICKS: #3 and KWAME look at him, #3 silently mouthing “Where *were* you?” They are sitting around an oblong table - oval on one side flat on the other which is placed up against a window looking through to the engineer's sound booth. There are newspapers, coffee cups, magazines, donuts etc., scattered all around

SPORTSCASTER (CONT'D)
Cassius, it's all you.

DJ
All right all right, Thank you and good morning. How's everybody feeling out there?

KWAME
I'm feeling like you late.

DJ
(ignoring him)
Now then if I remember right we always start off the morning with what? (points to engineer who hits promo tape)

RECORDED VOICE
(chorus of kids yelling) "Can I ask a Question?"

DJ
So for all you curious and precocious or just plain nosy folks out there, we back on line waiting on your calls so we can satisfy your unstoppable hunger to know things – no matter how trivial they always are – we are here for you like the Encyclopedia Brittanica.

KWAME
Or is that the Encyclopedia Ebonica?

#3
Or is it just a bunch of gossip folks with nothing better to do in the morning?

DJ
Whatever the weather, and however you like your toast buttered, we are here to let you ask whatever it is you just gotta know and let the people speak – from the controversial to the commonplace – from the gutter to the governator, this is freedom of speech. So get up on the soap-box and speak your piece.

KWAME
All right now, caller, you are on the air.

SPLIT SCREEN APPEARS FROM RT. SIDE TO TAKE UP HALF THE FRAME (THIS IS HOW ALL OF THE CALLERS WILL APPEAR ON SCREEN UNLESS NOTED OTHERWISE):

An ELDERLY BLACK WOMAN with a Sunday Church dress and reading glasses on a string of fake pearls lying on her chest with her hair pinned up in some complicated style speaks from her end of the telephone line

CALLER # 1 (ELDERLY BLACK WOMAN)
Hello? I got a question for y'all.

DJ
Go ahead.

CALLER #1
I was at my grand-daughter birthday party and they was handing out the cake, and of course my daughter she too lazy to take the time to make real whip cream, cause can't none of y'all cook no more, and so my question is I'm looking at my little baby girl eating up all this stuff they giving her, and I want to know, What exactly is Kool Whip?

KWAME
(not believing his ears) What is Kool Whip?

CALLER #1
Yeah, cause it been in the fridge for four month, and it ain't go bad and I'm looking at it going that ain't natural, so must be some kind of chemical make it stay that way, all bouncy and fluffy and stuff.

DJ
Sodium Caseinate.

#3
What?

DJ
Sodium Caseinate, that's what's in Kool Whip, that's what's in all non-dairy creamers.

CALLER #1
Now, what the –

#3
Now where you go pulling that out your hat?

DJ
Cause I read. I read the label, and if I don't like what I see, I don't eat it.

CALLER #1
Excuse me, excuse me, but what is that – Sodium Carbonate?

DJ
Dear it's Sodium Caseinate not Carbonate.

CALLER #1
OK, but what is that?

KWAME
(LH on Kwame)
How do you eat?

DJ
(LH of screen back to DJ)
Two words, my brother: Soul Food.

CALLER #1
EXCUSE ME! I thought this show was called "Can I ask a Question?" Right? So I got a question and y'all too busy yakking away to answer my question.

DJ
I'm sorry, dear. Actually I don't know what Sodium Caseinate is. So LA you heard the lady, we calling out to all mad scientists

in the city of Angels, we need to know what exactly is Kool Whip, you heard?
We're sorry darling, we just get carried away some times, but I'm sure we'll have an answer for you soon enough. Thank you for calling.
(cuts call) (split screen goes away)

Question is asked: Did President Crush sell drugs?

EXT. DUSTY ROADSIDE BAR - TIJUANA, MEXICO – DAY

CUT TO:

INT - SAME BAR - DAY

The WOMAN tending bar slides a beer and a shot of tequila down to a CUSTOMER who places a few crumpled pesos on the bar and leers at her. Cassius Timmons' show is on the radio over by the window.

CUT TO:

INT - CLOSE UP SHOT OF RADIO - DAY

Camera is focussed in on the old style transistor radio, covered in dust, surrounded by peanut shells and bottle caps. It is crackly with static, but you can definitely hear the DJ's voice continuing on with his morning's radio show. All you see is the radio filling the whole screen except for the dirty window pane behind it and maybe a part of a neon sign flickering.

DJ
(on radio speaker)
Well now who do we have next on the line?

PACO "SLOW-POKE" RODRIGUEZ
(in a voice slow as molasses)
Eh-speedy, tell them already, tell them.

RAMON "SPEEDY" GONZALEZ
(speaking real fast)
Eh! Am I on the radio?! This is Ramon. Is this where you asking all the any kinds of crazy retarded questions?

PACO "SLOW-POKE" RODRIGUEZ
Tell 'em Speedy, let 'em know!

CAMERA CUTS TO:

INT. RADIO STATION DJ BOOTH – DAY

DJ
Yessir, you are on the air. What question do you have for us?

CUT TO:

SPLIT SCREEN APPEARS PUSHING IN FROM LEFT HAND SIDE. SPEEDY AND SLOW POKE ARE THERE WITH THEIR FRIENDS WHO LOOK LIKE THEY'RE PART OF A MEXICAN HARLEY GANG, EXCEPT MOST OF THE BIKES ARE "INDIANS" INSTEAD OF HARLEYS

SPEEDY
Yeah, You gonna like this! I gotta good crazy retarded question for you.
(him and Slo-Poke and other bikers bust up laughing)

DJ
OK, OK, go ahead, what is your question?

SPEEDY
(laying on extra thick accent)
I wann to axe, (pausing - more laughing) I wann to axe is you President, and his President-Father before hinm plus both the Mrs. First Ladies of the Daughters of Plymouth Rock and the Boston Tea Party (more shouting and laughing) - Are they like big-time dealers OF NARCOTIC SUBSTANCES?
(room explodes with laughter)

Or WHAT?!!!
(room quiets down for a second)

SLO-POKE
(still all slow and molasses-like)
Yeahhhh, orrr whaad?

WHOLE BIKE GANG
(picks up chorus) (chanting together hopping up and down)
OR WHAT?!!! OR WHAT?!!! OR WHAT, OR WHAT, OR WHAT???!!!!

SPLIT SCREEN PUSHES DJ OFF THE SCREEN THIS TIME SO YOU CAN SEE A BUNCH OF FAT MEXICAN BIKER DUDES AND WOMEN ALL GATHERED AROUND SPEEDY AND SLO-POKE AT A PAY PHONE IN SOME OTHER MEXICAN ROADSIDE BAR AS THEY LOCK ARMS AND DANCE AROUND SHOUTING:

WHOLE BIKE GANG (CONT'D)
OR WHAT, OR WHAT, OR WHAT?!!!! YEEEEE! HEEEE!!!! WHOOOOOO!!!!! OR WHAT? OR WHAT? OR WHAT, OR WHAT, OR WHAT???!!!! AIYYYYY!!!!!! AIYY - AIYYY- YAIYY!!!!! You told 'em! Ha haiyyyyy aiyyyy aiyyyyyyyy!!!!!!!!!!!!!!!
(more dancing and jumping around)

Split screen pushes back to halfway as:

DJ
HOLD UP!!! HEYY!!!! HEYYYY!!!!
(looks at the ceiling because the bikers have got their momentum up and won't be interrupted)

Split screen pushes back to full on the bikers.

Beer bottles are flying and crashing into walls, a gun goes off several times in the street, a huge fat Mexican biker dude is plastered up against an even fatter Mexican womans wearing a Viking helmet, 2 other women in leather jackets are dancing flamenco on the bar, the bartender is steady pouring shots of whiskey as he ducks beer bottles.

WHOLE BIKE GANG
OR WHAT?!!!! OR WHAT?!!!!!! OR WHAT, OR WHAT, OR WHAT?!!!!!! WHEEEEEE HEEEEEEEEEE!!!!!!!!!!!!

CUT TO:

CLOSE UP OF SPEEDY WITH THE TELEPHONE ON HIS EAR, LISTENING AS:

DJ
HEYYYYYYY!!!!!!! HEYYYYYY!!!!!!!!!

CUT TO:

INT - ANOTHER, CLASSIER MEXICAN RESTAURANT - DAY
CUSTOMERS ARE CROWDED AROUND THE SPEAKER OF AN EXPENSIVE LOOKING STEREO LISTENING AND LAUGHING AS THE ECHOES OF:

WHOLE BIKE GANG
OR WHAT?!!!!! OR WHAT?!!!!!!! OR WHAT, OR WHAT, OR WHAT?!!!!!!!

mexxed with:

DJ
HEYYYYYY!!!!!! WHAT IS WRONG WITH YOU PEOPLE?

CUT BACK TO:

SPEEDY
(WHISTLES)
HEY EVERYBODY SHUDDUP!!!!! THE GRINGO WANT TO SAY SON-THING~!!!!!! SHUT UP ALREADY!!!!!!

DJ
Excuse me, what in God's Name are you talking about?!!!!

SPEEDY
(people are sill talking in background)
Eyyy!!!!! I tole you to SHUT UP, j'OK. I gotta talk now!!!
(people quiet down some)

DJ
Thank you! My God! Now what is this about?

SPEEDY
Sir, we are big-time Tierra Pistas in our country.

SLO-POKE
Speedy, I thought we suppose to be Professors.

SPEEDY
That's right, amigo, we are professors.

DJ
You're professors?

SPEEDY
From the university of MaMa Juana, and we are also industrialists on the board of directors of a big company of burning rubber.

DJ
Burning rubber?

SPEEDY
Jess. We burn rubber using sophisticated power transmissions equipment to provide energy for our children in the future all accross our state.

DJ
Where is this again?

SPEEDY
MaMa Juana - You may no know it. It is a small place - dark, very wet like a jungle, but very much beloved here in our country.

DJ
(chuckling a bit)
OK, Professors..... and what may I ask are you professors of?

SPEEDY
Natural history and geology - We are studying the history of the dirt.

DJ
The Dirt?

SPEEDY
As you know, sir, the earth and the dirt are the same exact thing. In Spanish it is only one word, so no confusion on this point.

DJ
And you said you were terra - whatsis?

SPEEDY
Tierra - pistas.

KWAME
Therapists?

SPEEDY
Son-thing like that. You gringos have some mental blockages about natural facts that happened in you past lifetimes. We are Tierra-Pistas - we know the real places you travel in you "bananas-republics" adventures on our soil. Real because we travel up and down the pista - the camino real, and we carry you bags to and fron' the planes - both the tourist plane and the private jet with diplomatic amnesia from insanity.

KWAME
Diplomatic immunity?

SPEEDY
Whatever.

DJ
OK, *doctors*, why are you calling us?

SPEEDY
Well we have been looking at your choices of who to run our economy next by remote control, and we not liking the selections and scenarios, and we also looking at certain - how you say? - key-lo sections of the underground economy coming accross in the Sealed Navy Envelopes from Afghanistan, and we somewhat no happy.

DJ
Yes and - ?

SPEEDY
And since you Mr. Nice Guy letting anybody get up and ask any kine question you wann.... We have - as fully-have-you-ever-been-experienced Semi-Professional Tierra-Pistas - scientifically formulated a question to open wider the legs of the no so esceptionally esmart President problems matrix

#3
You doing what?!!!!!!

SLO-POKE
We slinging mud at you eh-stupid President, heh-heh...

WHOLE BIKE GANG
More laughing and yelling.

SLO-POKE
EHHHH!!!!!! Shut up already - We talking to the Gringos!

#3
And what you doing that for? - Why you slinging mud at our President?

SLO-POKE
Cause he Mex-ing up our economy and pushing a whole lotta brown sugar on our kids.

ROSIE PEREZ LOOKING MEXICAN BIKER
That's why, pendejo!!!DJ
And by brown sugar you mean drugs?

SLO-POKE
By Brown Sugar I mean Heroin, papa, Afghanistainian heroin coming back from the war nobody wants!

ROSIE PEREZ LOOKING MEXICAN BIKER
And you trying to make our kids fight the war for you just so they can get Green Cards, asshole!

All the women crowd around "ROSA" slapping her hand and saying, "That's right!"

SPEEDY
OK, Yess Yess, but remember what we talk about: We got one question specially make for the Gringos to learn about who they is, j'OK?

DJ
Alright, so you got one question you want answered, right? And that one question is?

SPEEDY
Is you President of the United States George W. Crush and his super-Protestant #1 lady - Is they a part of a mafioso type Drug Dealing family that been pushing drugs onto little kids since all the way back to the 1950's -
(looks over at Slo-Poke, who looks back at him with a HUGE smile spreading over both their faces)

SPEEDY AND SLO-POKE TOGETHER
- OR WHAT?!!!!!!

WHOLE BIKE GANG
OR WHAT?!!!!! OR WHAT, OR WHAT, OR WHAT?!!!!!!!!!
(chorus picks up again stronger than before) OR WHAT?!!!!!
OR WHAT?!!!!! OR WHAT, OR WHAT, OR WHAT?!!!!!!!!

SPEEDY
This telephone gonna self-destruct in just a coupla seconds, j'OK?

DJ
WHAT?!!!!

SLO-POKE
DALE, CABRON!!!!!

WHOLE BIKE GANG
SI!!!! VAYA!!!!! DALE!

SPEEDY
(pulling big silver revolver)
Stan' back!!!!! (drops receiver) !Toma!!!!! (shoots payphone until coins spill out of coin slot)

SOUND OF DIALTONE

#3
Line's dead, Cassius.

DJ
All right that's fine. Good-bye!
(hangs up on call) (to himself:)
Did Crush deal drugs?
What in God's name do we do with this?

#3
Cassius this a joke, man. Some drunk Mexican dudes, let it go.

CUT TO:

FULL SCREEN: MEXICAN BIKE GANG REVVING UP THEIR BIKES AND PEELING OUT OF THE PARKING LOT.

SPEEDY
VAMONOS, LOCOS, VAMONOS!!!! ARRIBA! ECCCH BA!!! ECCH BA! WAAAA!!!!!!! (voice blends into the sound of loud tailpipes)

CUT TO:

INT RADIO STATION DJ BOOTH – DAY

DJ
Kwame, what you think of this? It's international territory, and you our international expert.

KWAME
Bwana, me no gwan' mek fe captain on dishwasher salary!!! You de captain, guide de ship, man, leave Kwame outta dis, man!

DJ
(shaking his head)
Not now, man, (to #3) Why every time (stabbing air for emphasis) we get something controversial, he got to go into that Patois shit!

#3
(throwing his hands up in exasperation)
Man, he on that African Hot Sauce again! Don't pay him no mind!

DJ
(looking up at sky)
Where do they come from? That's all I wanna know is where do these people come from?

KWAME
Bwana wan fe go shark fishing, guide dee boat, man!!! Kwame

BuShiDo

stay true, na neva jump ship, neva man!!!

DJ

Man, I need some music! Curtis! Man, get me some music!

MUSIC: "CISCO KID" - WAR (INSTRUMENTAL)

Chaos and Information – Looking for Ruppert

Radio Station lines are open.

EXT. – LA STREET SCENES – DAY

It's morning rush hour in LA and as the DJ takes calls, the camera moves with the beat of the music ("CISCO KID" (INSTRUMENTAL) - WAR) and the streets as we move past people having breakfast, playing dominos, traffic jams, tourist Hollywood, and gang spots where deals are already being made.

CALLER (LITTLE BLACK GIRL)

(split screen on her twirling the phone cord around her finger)

Is it really true that the President sold drugs? My Daddy says it is. He said that the Bloods and the Crips got all their drugs from the President. But I don't see how he could do all that and still have time to talk on the TV. Do you think he did it?

KWAME IS SHAKING HIS HEAD AND LAUGHING, #3 IS NOT AMUSED - SHAKING HIS HEAD AND MAKING SLASHING MOTIONS OVER HIS THROAT LIKE "CUT THIS", THE DJ IS JUST LOOKING UP AT THE SKY LIKE "WHY ME?"

DJ

I don't know, little girl

CALLER (LITTLE BLACK GIRL)

(annoyed)

I thought this was "Can I ask a question?"

DJ
It is, baby, we gon' do our best, but this isn't an easy question.

CALLER (LITTLE BLACK GIRL)
Cause why?

DJ
Cause it's controversial.

#3
Now go on to school where you belong and stop giving me a damn headache!

CALLER # 1 (LITTLE BLACK GIRL)
You ain't my daddy!

#3
If I was your daddy, I wouldn't be talking to you about no damn president selling no damn drugs to no damn gangs!!! Kids act like they know every damn thing! (imitating) "My daddy say" - Know what my daddy said? My daddy said shut up and get to school and stop acting so smart!!! Good-Bye!!!
(click - dial tone)

DJ
(laughing at #3's outburst)
Next caller, you on the air, what you got to say?

CALLER #10
(FLO FROM ALICE/MEL'S DINER)
You know, I have listened to your show for years, and generally I like y'all, because you are funny, but this is plain disgusting. You got no right to be talking trash about a man just because he is a public figure. Here you go listening to any dumb-ass who got 25 cents to make a phone call and start spreading all kinds of rumors and lies just so you can make a buck on some sensationalism and that ain't right. The president is a great man, and this is a great country and y'all should be thankful

to all the people who have fought to make this country the greatest country on earth instead of sitting on your backsides making up a bunch of filthy lies cause you ain't got nothing better to do. It's a damn shame.

DJ
Lady, I do apologize, but all I can tell you is I don't pick 'em, they pick me. Next caller, you're on the air. Did Crush deal drugs, yes or no?

CALLER #11 (WOODY HARRELSON)
Yeah fuckin A right he sold drugs. He was the director of the CIA during Viet Nam.

DJ
Wait, was that him or his father?

WOODY
What's the difference man, they're in the same family. You know tree don't fall far from the seed –

KWAME
– WHAT?! –

WOODY
You know what I mean. I mean they're all fascists, man, they're like Nazi sympathizers, you know? Half those guys in the CIA are like O.G.'s you know what that stands for? Original Gestapo. That's right baby, you ever hear of Operation Paper Clip? How about Special Agent Phillip Agee, he wrote a book all about it, man, it's all there – all you gotta do is go out and find it, man, or like how about how they went and made the most beautiful little plant – a plant that could save the world no lie – they went and made a plant illegal.

DJ
You're talking about weed?

WOODY
(looking upward with that look like "Thank God! Somebody finally gets it!")
Cannibus Sativa, baby, that's right! Did you know that Columbus sailed to the New World using hemp ropes and hemp sails? Did you know that? Or how about that George Washington grew weed on his farm? They all did, man. It's a fucking conspiracy man. All these Nazi sympathizers are like controlling the White House and the Media, and making war on America, putting people in jail for like growing a plant that could save the world, and then they went and made weed almost as expensive as cocaine, man. And there is no way that weed should be the same price as coke man. Coke takes like a whole garbage bag of leaves just to make an ounce and it is like really hard to grow – it only grows way up in the mountains in certain countries where like weed is natural and easier to grow than tobacco even. I mean a pack of 20 joints should cost less than a pack of 20 cigarettes.

DJ
Man get to the point! What are you saying?: Did Crush sell or didn't he?

WOODY
He most definitely did, sir. They all did, all those CIA freaks. They're like Nazi Mafia, man. They did it.

DJ
All right, thank you, your opinion has been noted. (hangs up) Whooo! Where do they get these people LA?. Next caller.

CALLER #12
(TRUCK DRIVER)
(Deep Country accent)
Hey, Cassius.

DJ
Hey, Hey is this who I think it is?

TRUCK DRIVER
Dang right it is. This is the Lone Ranger out here on the Lonesome Highway watching the Tumbleweeds fly by.

#3
(yelling)
Hey, where Tonto at?!

DJ
(ignoring him)
10-4 Lone Ranger, how you been old buddy?

TRUCK DRIVER
Just about as happy as you please cruising out here in the Oklahoma Panhandle

DJ
Wait a minute. How you picking us up?

TRUCK DRIVER
Got you streaming live on the internet, Breaker Breaker.

DJ
Well ain't you the cyberspace cowboy.

TRUCK DRIVER
That's a 10-4 good buddy.

DJ
So what you got to say about all this mess we hearing today. Break it down for me: Did he do it or didn't he?

TRUCK DRIVER
Well, you know I love your show, and so when I heard this, I just had to call in. Now we all seen that Michael Moore and his 9/11 piece a crap – scuse my French – that he called a documentary. And so now I guess people is thinking "Well, shoot I can make up some dirt about the President, too." But

BuShiDo
Cassius don't you believe none of it. I mean it's true about George Jr. having had a problem at one time as a young man with toot and all, you know back when he was in the National Guard, but when you're young and everybody's doing stuff, well, just like Bill Clinton did while he was in England, you know, George Jr. experimented, and me personally I don't think there's nothing wrong with that – it just shows he's human. And well Barbara his wife, being the good woman that she is well she come and brought him on through that rough patch in his life and now he's a good Christian, and he don't touch nothing, God bless him, which is more than I can say for Bill and Hillary Clinton – I mean talk about a messed up family over there, they're just out and out perverted. So that's the skinny good buddy, George had a problem and he faced it like a man and got over it with the help of the Almighty.

DJ
So you're saying this is all a bunch of nonsense?

TRUCK DRIVER
Don't believe a word these anonymous cowards are saying! If it weren't for the president's father fighting so hard to win the War on Drugs back in the 80's, things'd be in way worse shape than they are now. I mean we'd be flooded in all kinds of drugs. It's bad enough as it is, but if his father – God Bless Him – hadn't taken a tough stand – and I got a lot a buddies in jail for dealing because a him being tough, so it's not like I ain't felt the pain of this war we're fighting – but dammit right is right and the Crush's been on the right side of this fight from day numero uno. You know how it is man, these dealers will tear you a new one if you give em half a chance. Tough love is the only way to go, good buddy. Lock 'em all up and let God sort 'em out.

Well I gotta go weigh in and drain the main vein, so I hope that straightened your weed hopping conspiracy theorists on out. My friend if you're out there listening, I got 2 things to say to you: 1) get help, professional help and 2) Every once in a while it is the government, like that thing in Waco, Texas, the ATF was way outta line. But buddy, you are living in the greatest democracy on the face of the earth, the good old US of A, and if you're that mad about it why don't you go on over to China or Russia and see how you like it when you're starving to death and Mao can't even get you a bowl a rice let alone a pot to piss in, you hear me compadre?

DJ
I hear ya, big bear, stay under the radar, ya hear?

TRUCK DRIVER
This is the Lone Star Ranger over and out...

EXT - WHITE HOUSE – DAY

CUT TO:

INT - NATIONAL SECURITY COUNCIL OFFICES - DAY

MUSIC - SAME FOREBODING CELLO MUSIC FROM FIRST SCENE WITH NORTH

SUBTITLE: "NATIONAL SECURITY COUNCIL HEADQUARTERS 1981"

North is seated at desk scribbling with his pencil on memos that appear as overhead projections. Documents pertaining to the Executive Order signed by Ronald Reagan authorizing a Covert Operation in Nicaragua.

His intercom buzzes:

NORTH
Yes?

VOICE
Another applicant for the secretarial position, sir.

NORTH
What's the name?

VOICE
Fawn Hall, sir.

NORTH
Send her in.

CUT TO:

ESTABLISH PROFESSOR

THE OPIUM WAR – WHAT IT WAS; HOW IT PLAYED OUT; IS CHINA STILL MAD? (GOOD QUESTION, PEDRO)

INT. – PROFESSOR'S CLASSROOM – DAY

The PROFESSOR dressed in the elbow patches and Rex Harrison tweed coat, opens the door and addresses his bored looking class. In this scene, it looks like we're just walking in on a regular classroom at a college campus. No surreal effects just a blackboard and students with textbooks.

PROFESSOR
(looks down over his nose, assessing his new class of amateurs)
All right class, please open your textbooks to chapter 23, The Opium War
Now can anybody tell me from yesterday's class what the different kinds of warfare are? Anybody?
(writes on the blackboard)
there is Military, right?... Economic.... Chemical as in Poison Gas or the Defoliant Agent Orange.... and there is also a Drug War.
Teresa, What is a drug war?

TERESA
(a stereotypical blond cheerleader raising her hand with bright eyes and perfect posture)
That's like the war on drugs, right?

PROFESSOR
No, it is not a War on Drugs where they arrest drug dealers. Pedro?

PEDRO
(a Chicano stoner with his eyes hidden behind a pair of mirrored sunglasses)
I thought it was the war on drugs too. I don't know, bro.

PROFESSOR
(jabbing his hand to emphasize his points)
A DRUG WAR - people - is when drugs are used as a weapon - to destabilize a population. And the Opium War was waged against the people on the coast of China by England when they wanted to weaken China and take land and money and get better business deals by obtaining something called "Most Favored Nation Status." (pause).... And they weakened China by making the Chinese people addicts. They flooded the market with cheap Opium, and in the course of ten years thousands of Opium Dens opened up - (Pedro raises his hand) Yes, Pedro?

PEDRO
Is an Opium Den - is that like a Crack House?

PROFESSOR
Yes Pedro that 's like a Crack House. And from 1865 to about 1880 England moved in and supplied cheap Opium to thousands of these Opium Dens. At one point British War Ships actually attacked the Chinese fleet in order to assert their right to deal drugs in the ports. They won, and the Chinese as a people spent 100 years recovering.

TERESA
(popping her bubble gum)
How do you mean recovering?

PROFESSOR
Well the Chinese finally got back Hong Kong in 1991 - So from

1865 to 1991 is 125 years. And in some sense there is always some level of drug activity. Opium and heroin etc have been around for a long time, but the levels that existed during the Opium War were like an epidemic - a flood or perhaps more like a plague - a disease that was released into the atmosphere just like Agent Orange. It is like bombing a city - for years - and when you look at low income neighborhoods in our major cities - that is what you saw. People lost their homes, their cars, families were torn apart, homelessness went through the roof and people's immune systems became weakened. AIDS was another aspect. Addicts share needles - their immune systems are impaired. The heroin imported in the 1960's and 70's from Viet Nam, Laos, and Cambodia was like a wave of bombs hitting the neighborhoods. And the Crack Cocaine flood that followed was equally devastating. Pedro?

PEDRO

But all right then what do they call this drug war - the one from the 60's?

PROFESSOR

That - (pauses for effect) - is a good question.

INT - NORTH'S OFFICE - SAME DAY

As scene starts, there is a pause in the conversation. North has taken a moment and is just looking intently at Fawn Hall. He likes what he sees. He starts in again:

NORTH

We will be traveling together, working with the Freedom Fighters in El Salvador, Honduras, and Nicaragua, as well as with various operatives in the Middle East on both sides of the Iran-Iraq Conflict. You have to be able to devote yourself 110% to this job, and your loyalty will have to be unquestioning and without fail you will have to be totally dedicated to these 2 corresponding operations. Is that something you feel you can do?

FAWN HALL
(tilting head to one side quizzically)
Both sides of the Iran-Iraq conflict?

NORTH
(staring straight ahead, he looks piercingly into her eyes)
In this case, we are dealing with Security issues including the hostage situation in Lebanon, and our approach must be as flexible as possible. After all the terrorists aren't limited in the options available to them. We must do the exact same thing. I expect to be in the field quite a bit.

FAWN HALL
Then who will I be reporting to if you are in the field?

NORTH
You will report only to me. The White House must have absolute plausible denial capability on all levels, understood?

FAWN HALL
(camera close up on her lips only as she says)
I understand. (with just a touch of reverb)

It almost sounds sexy.

NORTH
(stares at her a long second)

CLOSE UP ON HIS EYES -- A VOICE IN HIS HEAD: -- "YOU LOOK LIKE FARRAH FAWCETT"

(snaps back to 2 shot)

NORTH (CONT'D)
Do you have any questions for me?

HALL
No, sir, I think I can do this job.

NORTH
That's great. We'll be in touch. Soon.

HALL
Well thank you very much for the chance. I've heard incredible things about you.

MUSIC STARTS IN THE BACKGROUND SOFTLY - BEACH BOYS (JUST THE INSTRUMENTAL) - "I WISH THEY ALL COULD BE CALIFORNIA GIRLS"

HALL (CONT'D)
You know my father served in Viet Nam?

NORTH
Really? What unit?

HALL
101st Airborne.

Their eyes meet for just a moment.

NORTH
Good unit.

HALL
Well I should let you get back to your work.

NORTH
Ms. Hall, a pleasure to meet you. As I said I'll be in touch soon. Have a beautiful day.

HALL
(looking back at him with more than a touch of warmth)
Thank you, sir.

She shakes his hand and walks out the door. Camera follows her as she walks down the hall and past other workers - it goes to slow motion, and she looks somewhat like a cross between a soldier in uniform and a runway model as the volume comes up: "I - wish - they - aalll - could - be - Cal - i - fornia - Girrrllls (Wish they all could be California)...

Sound of jet plane taking off that crescendos and then pounds like a gavel.

CUT TO:

EXT. - RURAL EL SALVADOR – DAY

A GROUP OF NUNS is walking through the central square of a small pueblo. There are donkeys swatting flies with their tails and chickens scratching at the dusty earth.

CUT TO:

They arrive at a small building and enter. Inside a group of wounded people are laid out on cots and blankets. They slowly begin the work of ministering to their wounds and changing dressings etc.

ESTABLISH ERNESTO – YOU KILLED MY TIA THE NUN

EXT. OUTSIDE A MIDDLE CLASS HOUSE IN EL SALVADOR – DAY

ERNESTO, a young Salvadoran college student is standing staring at his UNCLE who is seated under the shade of a tree in their backyard looking up at Ernesto with a sympathetic but somewhat confused expression on his face

ERNESTO
I will go to Jollywood and make them a movie and showet them what they did to Tia!

UNCLE
Primo, they wonn belief you, you have no money, you got no connections.

ERNESTO
I have the 2000 dollars for the school.

UNCLE

Primo, 2000 dollars wont get you any thing not even an apartment in Jollywood for 3 months. No food. Nothing. Here you can go to school for a year and write a book.

ERNESTO

A book won't do anything. Asturias already said everything and nobody up there even know him. It have to be a movie. It have to be Jollywood.

UNCLE

Primo, nobody in Jollywood is going to listen to your shit, OK? Nobody. There is no way they gonna give a movie to a Spic about what happens here, man. Write a book or go to Mexico City and make a movie there.

ERNESTO

What about Banderas? He makes movies in Jollywood every year.

UNCLE

Banderas makes movies about gangsters shooting everywhere killing eachother for money, and it's all fake. Banderas makes Zorro. You want to make a movie about nuns getting killed by the fucking Marines, man. They going to shoot you like they shoot Tia. Primo, if they shoot her, what is it to kill you, man, it's nothing to them.

ERNESTO

No, in United States they don't shoot people. The marines only do it here and in other countries, Panama, or Chile, in Africa, not in LA, they don't shoot people.

UNCLE

What are you talking about, primo? They gonna put some bag of drugs in you pocket and fucking say you were a drug dealer resisting arrest. Man, stop playing games and look at reality, man, cause they're not playing.

ERNESTO
No, you look at reality. Tia is dead. You gonna see. I gonna make a movie, but it's going to be different. I'm going to make a Japanese movie in Jollywood about what happen in El Salvador, and you going to see it. Then they can fucking shoot me, but they gonna see wh'appen with Tia. They gonna see what they do. They the ones selling the drugs, and they the ones who shot Tia, and Tia didn't do anything.

CUT TO:

Ernesto taking off at midnight on his motorcycle passing a sign:

Mexico 1300 km

INT. RADIO STATION – LA – DAY

THE BIN LADEN CONNECTION

DJ
You are on the air. What you got to say?

CALLER
So yes. I have been watching some news and I see one thing very clear. We are not paying any attention to Saudi Arabia, and this is very important. Listening to the reporters all day going on and on about Iraq and Iran, but they never say anything bad about the Saudi Arabia. And this is not accurate. Saudi Arabia is putting a lot of money into private armies, and Osama bin Laden is from Saudi Arabia not Iraq or Iran and supposedly the bin Laden Family is the one who started the war in Middle East. They are also the one in the Fahrenheit 9/11 movie that put everything into the original Crush business of flying the planes and I am only guessing but I think that the Bin Laden Family was provoking terrorism all the way back then by drastically increasing the importation of Cocaine in partnership with the Crush Family. I can be wrong, but

this is something that makes sense if you look closely at the Fahrenheit 911 movie.

DJ
So you think Saudi Arabia is part of the problem?

CALLER
No Saudi Arabia, it is the Bin Laden Oil Family and well not all of Saudi Arabia. That is like saying all of the United States or all of California. But yes in the movie there is a part where they talk about a partnership between George Crush and the Bin Laden's in an airplane company, and it was during the same time...

DJ
And what is your theory?

CALLER
Man I don't have any more than what was in the movie, and I don't want to make theories on that. It's not important really who it was, but the fact that we never talk about Crush dealing, right? Well we also never talk about Saudi Arabia and terrorism - not that I want us to add any more countries to the list, OK? - but we are leaving out the country where the bin Ladens live and that seems strange since we started the war because of bin Laden in the first place, no?

DJ
So no reason as to why?

CALLER
No, that's all I got to say.

DJ
Thank you caller for that, and who do we have next, caller, you're on the air.

CALLER 2
I want to say something quick and simple. Bin Laden own

all the Gum Arabic that make sticking the Caffeine with the caramel. That is what making the Coca Cola happen.

#3
I do not believe the kind of shit I hear in here these days!

DJ
Anything else you wanted to add to that, sir?

CALLER 2
That's all.

DJ
Well thank you. My God, where do they come from?

#3
I'm saying.

DJ
You heard the man?

#3
I don't know what some people are thinking! (shakes his head to clear the air) And you know, I can live with that.

DJ
I'm saying... Next caller.

(Hank Williams, Sr. Joint)

HANK WILLIAMS, SR
Now look, in World War 2, the I – talian drug dealers – meaning Lucky Luciano and his boys – risked their lives to help us beat the I – talian fascists – meaning your Mussolini followers.
Neither one of those 2 groups was really very nice when you get right down to it, but that was sort of the choice.
That all seems pretty minor and irrelevant right now, but back in World War 2 when people had to go bum-rush a machine

gun nest just to make it possible for their platoon to get up a hill literally covered in dead bodies, well it meant a whole heck of a lot for someone to become your blood brother in combat. And that was some of the nastiest combat the world has ever seen.
So it was a serious reason why Italian gangs received some government lookaway and favors. Lots of dirty deals get made in War Time, son.
I agree with what you're doing, but I'm just letting you know you're stirring up some big trouble. I gotta go...

DJ
(rolling his eyes)
O - K ....Next caller. Hi you're on the air.

DEEP COUNTRY
Hey How you doing, Mr. Timmons?

DJ
Just fine, sir. How are you, Mr. ahh – ?

DEEP COUNTRY
You can call me Deep Country.

#3
What?!

DEEP COUNTRY
You ever heard of that feller they called Deep Throat that helped bring down the Nixon Boys back in '72? Well, that man was Republican, and so am I. Modesty prevents me from telling you my real name, so you can just call me Deep Country, OK?

#3
Oh, hellll no!

DJ
OK, Deep Country, talk to me. What you got to say?

DEEP COUNTRY
Well you boys are definitely working on one of the right questions to ask, and with just a bit of digging, you going to get your answer, and we need you to expose these rats for who they are.

DJ
So you think he did it?

DEEP COUNTRY
What I think don't mean diddly squat. What matters to us and our grandkids is if people still care enough about this great country to want to know the truth. The truth is what makes us free. Otherwise, we're just slaves to the mass media, and it's no different than Russian propaganda. Now Watergate was an example of where 2 reporters bucked the system to uncover the truth. They risked everything and got no sleep till they traced that mess all the way to the top. They risked both their reputation as newspapermen, and their carreers and kept digging for months, working and working until they connected Nixon di-rectly to the money laundering and di-rect violations of the 4th amendment. Regarding what was called in the time of the Revolutionary War, the Inalienable Right to Privacy of a Citizen in their home or place of business.

DJ
OK...

DEEP COUNTRY
Now when Richard Nixon placed illegal wiretaps in the Democratic National Headquarters during a presidential election, he was in violation of the highest law of the land – the Constitution. The Bill of Rights is what makes this country great and what seperates us from England and France. Am I right sir or did I miss something in civics class?

DJ
Yes sir, I agree. Now please can you make your point?

DEEP COUNTRY
Pardon me sir. I don't want to take up your time or that of the listeners any more than I have to.
My point is this: The President of the United States takes a solemn oath with his hand on the bible to uphold the laws of this country. Especially the Constitution and the Bill of Rights. When Nixon rigged that election in 1972 using those wire taps, he was no longer the President, the Commander in Chief, or a Patriot. He was a traitor, just like Benedict Arnold. He was destroying the essence of Democratic Elections. He was undermining the very Constitution it was his sworn duty to defend with his life if necessary.
Now, what these Crush boys out of New England are doing –

#3
Wait a minute. I thought Crush was from Texas?

DEEP COUNTRY
If he's from Texas, how come he went to Yale University? Huh? How come he got a mansion in Maine? You take my word for it, George Crush is from New England. He is as blue blood as they come. Now as I was saying, what these Crush Boys are doing with the CIA and their National Security Police State bull hockey makes wire taps and campaign slush funds look like child's play. They are selling this country 10 cents on the dollar to foreign banks, they are violating the first, second, and fourth amendments, and they are engaging in monopoly anti-trust violations including Enron and bigger...

DJ
But are they selling drugs?

DEEP COUNTRY
(chuckling)
I'm going to leave that one to you, Mr. Cassius Timmons of Los Angeleze, C – A. The answers are all there, if you ask the right questions. Your question is "Did George Crush sell drugs, right?"

DJ
That's right.

DEEP COUNTRY
I got another one for you.

DJ
Which is?

DEEP COUNTRY
Did John Query help him?

DJ
Senator John Query from Massachusetts?

DEEP COUNTRY
Yup.

DJ
George Crush's opponent in the last election?

DEEP COUNTRY
Yup.

DJ
So you're saying not only did George Crush sell drugs, you're saying John Query helped him?

DEEP COUNTRY
I'm not saying anything. I already know more than is healthy for a man in my position to say. It's a free country, right? So like you said, Can I ask the question?

DJ
And your question is "Did Senator John Query help George Crush to run drugs?"

#3
Aww, hell no!!!

DJ
And you ain't going to help me answer it?

DEEP COUNTRY
Sometimes, Mr. Timmons, knowing what question to ask is half the battle. But I do have a hint for you.

DJ
What?

DEEP COUNTRY
Three card monty.

#3
What?!

DJ
You mean like the little street hustle?

DEEP COUNTRY
That's right. You two are men of the world. If you want a clue in your search, think about how you play that little game of confidence. If you need more help, I'll call again – but like I said I love a good fox hunt. Good luck! (click.)

#3
Aw hellls no!

DJ
Well, LA, you heard the man – we are officially in the Twilight Zone. Get at me, we drifting on the high plains of conspiracy now...

MUSIC: "WORD UP" - CAMEO

ERNESTO ARRIVES GUADALAJARA

INT. COLLEGE BAR – GUADALAJARA – NIGHT

HISPANO-GITANO COMMENTARY SECTION

MANA #1

(A Student at the University of Mexico - Guadalajara)
(smoking a cigar while he gestures with his hands)

(in Spanish) First you had them saying we were communists, no? Then, they said that we were drug dealers, and now they say we're terrorists. But when they come to visit us, we're still the same, and we invite them to sit down to and meet us and have dinner. And they like us, then when we cook them dinner, no? Escept they want us to move faster when we serve them. Then they go home and they send soldiers. Not because we're communists or terrorists, but because they want us to make them tennis shoes for $8/day. That's why, and we know it. They want us to grow them coffee and bananas and cocaine and marijuana all for $8/day, and then they want to believe that we come across their border and force them to buy all this cocaine at gunpoint. Like we running the drug business. Ask my grandfather, they wasn't even knowing how to make cocaine till the Germans got here and show them. And us controlling their cities, come on man, we can't even run things in our own country. The gringos put in all the presidents down here. They approve the senators and the cabinet. They put the generals on the CIA payroll. How the hell are we going to go up to their country and run things and become mafia bosses. The English and the Germans are the number one mafia, and they control the Washington DC. Then the Irish came and they got some control over the big cities mayor and the police in New York and Boston and Chicago. Then the Italians came, and they control the gambling and the prostitutes and selling on the streets and the garbage. How are we going to control the drugs in United States? We don't control the drugs, they want the drugs. They the ones was using all the drugs. We never make a cocaine man. Cocaine don't even grow here, it's down south, and the Indians down there they only chew like 5 or 10 leaves. They say it feels like a cup of coffee. You know how much it takes to make a little nothing gram of coke? A whole garbage bag of leaves. A fucking garbage bag. You couldn't

chew that many leaves if you started at 5 AM and kept chewing straight through to sunset. You know how much to make just one ounce of Coke? 8 garbage bags...
They don't give us no money for that. You know how much they selling a kilo of Coke in Bolivia, man? Little Pesos. You know how much that go for in United States? Big Dollars. Do the math. We don't have no army with weapons like they got. If we go to take control of Chicago, they will send the army, man. In the movie, they say we killed one of the fucking cabinet members of the US President. WHEN?! When we ever kill one of their presidents or Secretary of State or Generals or Senators or Nobody. We never kill nobody in they government, but they make it like we killed Big Shot people like that all the time. But United States did kill Presidents and Mayors and Senators down here. And how many they killed in Panama in one week? They killed hundred thousands in El Salvador. Hundred thousands, man. That's like having the World Trade Center bombing happen every day for like one year and a half maybe. They killed too many on Nicaragua. We never killed even one thousand of them. Man, Bin Laden killed 4,000, and they lost they minds and kill more than 100,000 in Iraq. For 2 years they killing people not even from Bin Laden country. And they want to tell us we killers and all this craziness? Imagine us looking at 5,000 dead every day. Imagine your 9/11 happening every day for a month straight, you turn on the TV and bombs are falling on you kids! You say that we are terrorists, but who makes more killing, who makes more terror, eh? You think we don't know your president is a liar in United States, that you pretend that we are the drug dealers and the terrorists. But look at the facts man. Who killed all those people in Panama? Who killed 200,000? That was the USA terrorists – the Christian Fanatics, man, say what you want, but we know the truth. We know the truth with our own eyes, with our own hearts. Nobody ever provoke you, you came to make business, to make us work for $8/day.

That is fucking truth, and you make war on us for that reason – not for communism or for terrorism or for all kinds of –ism – you make people die because they want a good pay for a good work just like you want. How you gonna say we are communists when we going to church more than you do? You kill people – lots and lots of people, so they afraid, and they work all day even they don't have money for school for their kids, and they don't have money to build a house. OK. You the boss. I see that. But don't come here with your bullshit about terrorism and communism and we are the drug dealers. You are the drug dealers, you are the big mafia bosses, and if you knew anything other than stupid news papers and Tom Clancy novels and Harrison Ford movies, you would know this and I wouldn't have to tell you."

GUADALAJARA PARTY

INT. – UNIVERSITY OF MEXICO – GUADALAJARA
CAMPUS BAR

The bar is packed, as Ernesto makes his way through the crowd, The music is bumping and vendors on the back patio are selling all kinds of tacos and gorditas, etc, and lots of beer. Dance Floor is standing room only, all the couples a bit happy and sweaty from the opening act. Just as he gets to the table where Mana is hanging out waiting for him, BAM! The spotlight kicks in and there is CELIA CRUZ,

CELIA CRUZ
Bienvenidos todo el mundo aqui en la plaza central de la Raza, barrio Tres Culturas, Estado Nativo, Mundo Mestizo. A todos mis companeros, te felicito. DALE!

The orchestra – maybe 20 deep – waits on the drummer who beats out a quick 2-3-4 and they fly into a Cumbia and the whole place starts dancing. And 2 seconds later somebody comes up and asks Ernesto to dance, and he's on the floor.

CUT TO:

PROFESSOR – HOW MUCH IS A LOT?

The Professor – still in his white lab coat – now walks down a dock past containers and pallet jacks and cranes, with his class in tow. They reach the end of the pier, and walk on board a cargo container ship where a set of chairs has been set up in the mammoth cavern of the empty hold, along with either an overhead projector or a computer projector or maybe a big easel with illustrations on cardstock.

PROFESSOR
So Pedro, why are we here?

PEDRO
(whistling - impressed by the size of it)
Cause it's cool! Hey man, how much can one of those cranes

lift?

PROFESSOR
Teresa? Why here?

TERESA
(teacher's pet voice)
To illustrate the size of the quantity of the amount of drugs that get imported every year.

PROFESSOR
Precisely. I call this lecture: "How much is a lot?"

PEDRO
(to Francois)
Dude this place is huge! Can you imagine what kind of a offshore grow room me and my cousins could make in here? We could do like the Amazon Rainforest, you know with like levels and overhead sprinklers -

FRANCOIS
- And you can power zee entire operayzhun with the diesel generators and no one could monitor your power output. You could operate in international waters so that you would be beyond ze jurisdigzhun of all the governemants of ze world... (Swears in French) Sacre Merde!

PROFESSOR
(ignoring them - walks to center of hold)
People like to imagine a very weird combination of scenarios when it comes to what may be 3 of the 20 largest crops in the United States economy and perhaps 3 of the top 5 money earners as well. But in many ways, marijuana, cocaine, and heroin are cultivated, harvested and shipped to market just like corn or soybeans or cotton. The main difference is that while corn goes for 35 cents a pound, wholesale and cotton for 2 dollars a pound, wholesale marijuana weighs in at $450/pound, wholesale Cocaine at $10-15,000/pound, and Heroin wholesales at $12-20,000/pound. I say that is the

most important difference because that is what drives the market – the price. Supply and Demand are the same for legal and illegal crops, except that being illegal drives the price up considerably. Being illegal it is argued also reduces the supply – one of the factors leading to the exceedingly high prices. But the high prices also act as a huge incentive to people to get in the business of growing and transporting these crops. These prices and the huge profits involved make the sale of illegal drugs big business.

Today, class, we are going to look at just how big the Drug Business is. Now we are dealing with illegal merchandise, and as a result we are dealing with a lower degree of accuracy in the range of the estimates. However, we can still get a decent concept of the size of the market as long as we are willing to accept a wider range of data. What that means is that we will be dealing with a larger gap between the lowest possible amounts consumed every year and the highest possible, but just like with any crop, when we know the approximate acreage in cultivation, then we know with a reasonable certainty how much is being produced. Now, given the fact that people are actively hiding their crops, it is more likely that our estimates are too low, rather than too high.

TERESA

Professor, how did you get your estimates?

PROFESSOR

Mexican Libraries.

TERESA

Mexican Libraries?

FRANCOIS

Professor, do you know if ziss boat is available for ze leasing or perhaps zee rental?

Lockheed C-130 *Hercules*

Type: Transport

Dimensions: wingspan, 132 feet, 7 inches; length, 97 feet, 9 inches; height, 38 feet, 3 inches
Weights: empty, 76,469 pounds; gross, 175,000 pounds
Power plant: 4 × 4,591-horsepower Allison T56 turboprop engines
Performance: maximum speed, 374 miles per hour; ceiling, 33,000 feet; maximum range, 4,894 miles
Armament: none
Service dates: 1956–

The *Hercules* is one of the most famous, most versatile aircraft ever built and flown. It has compiled four decades of distinguished service—and its best years are yet to come.

By 1952 the Air Force was seeking to update its tactical airlift capabilities by adopting its first turboprop-powered transport. Lockheed was awarded a contract, and the prototype XC-130 rolled out in 1955. It represented a radical departure in transport design by possessing a shoulder-mounted wing and an inclined cargo door at the rear of the fuselage. The capacious cargo hold was also completely pressurized and air-conditioned for ease of work. Moreover, the new craft was fully capable of landing on rough, unprepared landing strips under battlefield conditions. Despite the new plane's size, pilots reported that it was "built like a truck and handled like a Cadillac." It went into service with the Air Force as the C-130 *Hercules* in 1956; since then more than 2,000 have been built. In every respect the aircraft has lived up to its legendary name.

The variety of tasks assigned to the *Hercules* is staggering. It can haul passengers or paratroopers, perform aerial refueling, search-and-rescue, electronic warfare, and communications work. It was both the first large transport to be equipped with skis for work in the Antarctic and also the first four-engine plane to both land on and take off from a carrier deck. Naturally, this capable craft was sought out by the Navy, Marine Corps, and Coast Guard, each of which operates hundreds of its own specialized versions. Furthermore, the *Hercules* has been widely exported abroad and is operated by no less than 24 different countries. With continuous engine and avionics upgrades, the mighty C-130 will be a prime tactical transport for several more decades. One of the greatest aircraft ever.

AIRPLANES – 1960s

- 185 -

PROFESSOR
(deadpan)
I'll ask Francois.
Now, from what we know, there has been an explosive increase in drug production starting about ten years after World War 2. In 1958, Burma was exporting approximately 18 tons of opium, by 1970 that number had jumped more than 30 times to 600 tons. In Afghanistan we see the numbers skyrocket. 100 tons of opium in 1971 becomes 2,000 tons by 1991, and after the recent war with Afghanistan it increased to 4,600 tons. Marijuana is a bit more difficult to calculate for 2 reasons. One, much of the marijuana consumed in the US is grown in the US, primarily in the Mid-West and the Dirty South.

PEDRO
Did you say the "Dirty South?"

PROFESSOR
I did.

TERESA
So but professor, what is this all about?

PROFESSOR
You'll see in just a minute. Lights, please.
As the lights dim, the projector whirs to life and we see (perhaps plastered right on the whole movie screen):
What this means is simply this. People have imagined that somehow drugs come over our borders in a clandestine manner using a whole range of bizarre and impractical modes of transportation. Many movies postulate that significant quantities of drugs get from point A to point B using individual carriers who smuggle the drugs in balloons that they swallow or that they insert up their rectum.

TERESA
Ewwww!

PROFESSOR
You are about to see just how impossible it would be to move the quantities of drugs we are talking about in that manner.
First slide please.
This is approximately what 5,000 tons of opium would look like loaded into containers on a dock to be transported by ship.
Next slide, please.
Here we see a young man at the airport, lets call him "The Mule" He has a set of 20 balloons which we see here in front of him containing a grand total of 3 ounces of heroin. Now, if we assume that heroin is entering the country only by way of "Mules" such as this man, then it would take the entire population of Mexico 2 trips apiece to get all the Heroin into this country. That would mean over 200 million Mexicans, including mothers, grandmothers and small children, all sticking balloons in their ass 2 times a year, knowing that if a balloon breaks that they would instantly die of an overdose. Not exactly an efficient or a very clandestine way of conducting business.

PEDRO
Is that true the part about dying of an overdose if the balloon breaks?

PROFESSOR
Unfortunately, Pedro it is.
Now. Taking a more logical approach to a multi-billion dollar a year business, if you loaded it all on containers on ships like this one - next slide please - this is how many containers you would have to use to move the estimated quantities we're talking about: Slide, please.

The slide shows a bar graph representation of cargo containers (little pictures of cargo boxes) placed side by side showing how many it would take for Marijuana, Cocaine, and Heroin and below it little cargo ships showing how many fit in each ship.

PROFESSOR (CONT'D)
Now another way that is equally common for getting a crop to

market is the semi tractor trailer. Slide please.

Same thing with little pictures of 18 wheelers.

PROFESSOR (CONT'D)
As you can see we are not talking about a small import business. Now moving right along to another common mode of transport we come to everybody's favorite: Planes. There are 2 styles that are generally popular, the single prop Cessna and Lockheed's C-130 Hercules transport cargo plane. Slide please: As you can see, the C-130 has about double the capacity of a typical tractor trailer with the added advantage that the product can generally be loaded on without going to the trouble of hiding the contents since it is assumed that take off and landing will be at an appropriately secret location far from any customs inspectors.

Slide. (Cigarette Boat)

PROFESSOR (CONT'D)
Here we have an interesting favorite in the mythology: The Cigarette boat famous as being the only boat that can supposedly outrun the Coast Guard cutters and the Navy. While it is true that the boats are fast, it is also true that both the Coast Guard and the Navy have helicopters fast enough to eat even the fastest Cigarette boat up for breakfast. The other problem as we see here is that they just don't carry that much payload. As it turns out for cigarette boats to do the whole job of transporting these crops would require one boat to leave Cuba or Puerto Rico every 15 minutes between 10 pm and 8 am, and even then that doesn't account for how the crops would get from South America to Puerto Rico since Cigarette boats just don't have the range to cross from the Northern Caribbean to Columbia (slide showing distance from PR to Miami vs distance from PR to Columbia (on a map). So as you can see Cigarette boats although very sexy are not what you call practical.

Slide. (rusty Toyota 1.8)

PROFESSOR (CONT'D)
Now for fun I had these next couple drawn up. Just because people want to know. First off here we have the favorite car of Mexico – the Toyota Corolla. It is practical, cheap, and good on gas. Now even if we were to assume that you were brave enough to load pure product straight in the trunk with no worries about being arrested, this is how many trips it would take to move the annual imports to the US. Slide please
As you can see, it would be a serious parade. Using cargo vans

(slide showing a 74 Dodge Conversion Van with fringe and a shrine to the Virgin)

PROFESSOR (CONT'D)
even with no fear of being caught it would still take this many:

(slide)

PROFESSOR (CONT'D)
Moving right along, if you wanted to move it all by mule train

(slide)

PROFESSOR (CONT'D)
this is the size of the Mule train, and finally if we are talking about the nervous guy with indigestion and 20 balloons stuck up his ass – the modern day version of the Mule – this is how many people would have to perform that rather heinous act and risk the possibility of death.

PEDRO
Professor, did you say heinous?

PROFESSOR
I did.

CUT TO:

INT - SPANISH RESTAURANT - DAY

CHUCHI
(wearing a captain's hat, seated at a table talking to 2 tourists)
You wanna know how I know?
Noriega, that's how.
The whole time Crush is fighting his big-time War on Drugs, killing thousands of people with bombs and throwing maybe a million people in jail, who was his best friend in Latin America? Noriega.

And Crush isn't stupid. You don't get to be the Director of Central Intelligence by not knowing who's who.
Naw, man. If Crush didn't like drug dealers, then why did he take Manuel Noriega – who was a drug dealer since forever – why did Crush take Noriega and put him in charge of Panama and the Panama Canal where all the drugs is moving in those ships. He could have put some hard ass in charge of Panama – and if he really wanted to cut off the drug flow that was the place to do it – the key to the whole traffic – the Canal is like a bottleneck and everything moves through Panama to get here.

(Chuchi picks up a paper place mat with a map of Central America printed on it.)

Here come here! Look at the map. Here's Colombia and here's Bolivia growing all that Coke. Now look at Panama, it's the bottleneck. You want to cut off Bolivia and Colombia and all those drugs – this is where you do it. Right here. And who does he put? Noriega. And what happens to imports? They go from 80 tons a year, which is a lot already – to over 600 metric tons man, exactly during the time this mother is supposedly fighting a billion dollar war to stop it.
That's why I know. OK?

ESTABLISH RUPPERT - RUPPERT CALLS RADIO STATION

CALLER
Hi, is this Cassius Timmons?

DJ
Yes, sir, what can I do for you?

CALLER
Well, I heard you were looking to find out about the movement of Cocaine in US Government airplanes. Is that correct?

DJ
We did have someone ask the question. And that's what we're here for. Conspiracy theories are us.

CALLER
Well, in this case, I think you could call it a real live conspiracy - as in the RICO Act.

DJ
And how do you know this?

CALLER
Well, my name is Michael Ruppert and I was an LAPD Narcotics Detective.

#3
Hold - the - line! (bleep!) Yo!

DJ
Wait a minute. You're a cop?

MICHAEL RUPPERT
I was a cop. Past tense.

DJ
(surprised up out of his chair)
Wait a minute, wait a minute, - you're serious.

MICHAEL RUPPERT
Yessir, I am.

KWAME
And you think it happened?

MICHAEL RUPPERT
It happened a bunch of times.

#3
Yo! - Yo! Wait! Yo!

DJ
HOLD ON! Are you willing to go on the record about this?

MICHAEL RUPPERT
I have my own website.

#3
(laughing)
He got a website yo!

KWAME
Impressive.

DJ
Do you want to do an interview?

MICHAEL RUPPERT
I would love to.

DJ
I want to meet you. Can we do that? Can you come to the radio station?

MICHAEL RUPPERT
That's fine with me.

DJ
Alright. Hold on a minute. Don't go nowhere, (to #3) Man, put some music on! Lemme talk to this man!

CUT:

MUSIC: THE ROOTS - GIVE IT HERE (DON'T SAY NOTHING) b/w "YOU WANT PURE ENLIGHTENMENT - I'M DROPPING IT" (RED ALERT REMIX) --> "You have a very very very short attention span.... knowledge on the loose and there's no stopping it - you want true enlightenment? Well, I'm dropping it...."

Act II: Can I Get a Witness?

MUSIC: "NEEDLE AND THE DAMAGE DONE" – NEIL

YOUNG (EVERY JUNKIE'S LIKE A SETTING SUN)

FLASHBACK: DJ SEES SISTER DIE OF OD

SISTER'S FUNERAL

DJ'S FATHER BEATS HELL OUT OF DJ WITH BELT.

MUSIC: STEVIE WONDER "GANGSTER'S PARADISE"

Before Cassie dies, a soldier is hit by a mortar in VietNam.

Helicopter takes him back.

Operating room.

As soldier is taken out and put in body bag, heroin is processed and put in a kilo bag and then loaded into an empty ammo box.

Solider is shipped home in a transport plane, And on same transport plane, a pallet of the same ammo boxes is brought in on a forklift possibly wrapped with some shrink wrap and marked "Do not tamper" "Hazardous Material."

The plane takes off and then is shown landing at an Air Force base in Viet Nam.

The pallet is shown being loaded Into the hold of a freighter.

The soldier's body is transferred to another plane.

CUT TO:

INT - FUNERAL HOME – DAY

Mother and Father are crying over son in uniform.

CUT TO:

Cassie going out the door with two of her friends, dressed for school. Waves good-bye in slow motion.

CUT TO:

Mrs. Timmons bent over her daughter's body, her body racked by sobs as paramedics take Cassie away on a stretcher.

CUT TO:

REVEREND TIMMONS
(is beating Cassius with his belt)
God as my witness, (Slap!) if I EVER (slap!) see you hanging around (slap!) that block, I WILL (slap!) (breathing hard from exertion of beating his son) KILL (slap!) YOU (slap!) MY OWN (slap!) DAMN (slap!) SELF! DO YOU HEAR ME! DO YOU! (SLAP! SLAP! SLAP! SLAP!) DO YOU!

CASSIUS
(crying) Yes, sir! -

REVEREND TIMMONS
DO YOU!

MRS TIMMONS
STOP! STOP! YOU'RE KILLING HIM! STOP!

REV TIMMONS
(roaring) You stay the hell out of my way! Softness just took one of my children and I'll be God Damned if I sit around waiting for it to take another!

CUT TO:

INT - FUNERAL HOME - DAY

MUSIC: Gospel hymn

Eulogy is delivered. (With no sound only the gospel music.)

CUT TO:

CASKET IS LOWERED INTO GROUND AND DIRT IS THROWN ON TOP.

RUPPERT'S BIOGRAPHY

[NOTE: EVERYTHING HIGHLIGHTED BELOW WILL BE CONNECTED AS A SERIES OF IMAGES SHOWN WITH THE MUSIC: "ONLY LOVE CAN BREAK YOUR HEART" - NEIL YOUNG. THIS IS A FAST OVERVIEW OF RUPPERT'S LIFE AND BUSH'S HISTORY IN CENTRAL AMERICA..]

SEG-WAY: ONLY LOVE CAN BREAK YOUR HEART - NEIL YOUNG MUSIC IS PLAYING OVER AN ACCELERATED MONTAGE OF IMAGES:

RUPPERT GRADUATES POLICE ACADEMY.

INT. LOS ANGELES POLICE ACADEMY GRADUATION CEREMONY - DAY

A loudspeaker is booming the names of the GRADUATES as they come forward to receive their diplomas. Over the music you can hear the MASTER OF CEREMONIES call, "Michael Ruppert". There is a close up of Ruppert accepting diploma, and then a shot of his parents cheering and taking photos.

EXT - THE RUPPERT FAMILY'S BACKYARD - GRADUATION PARTY - DAY

There are picnic tables and barbecues full of food as RELATIVES AND FRIENDS mill around, Michael is there talking with them.

INT - SQUAD ROOM - DAY

Music lowers in volume considerably as Ruppert and FELLOW OFFICERS are given their daily briefing.

EXT. LOS ANGELES ALLEYWAY - DAY

Ruppert participates in a bust on a Crack House. Among those he arrests is A CRACKHEAD GIRL. He then takes her to rehab where there are another 100 in the same condition and a waiting list a mile long.

Shot 1: Police seen from behind a ways down the alley including the adjacent street, along with Vans and Squad Cars.

Shot 2: Above police centered on door. Police are wearing vests and helmets. They are about to use the battering ram to cave in the door.

Shot 3: Close Up of hole in door where drugs are dealt.

Shot 4: directly behind police and opposite as Sargent signals with hand "1-2-3" and batterring ram busts down door. Camera follows as police rush in. People screaming and running. Close up in bathroom as product is flushed away. Muted yelling ("Only Love Can Break Your Heart" still playing.)

CRACKHOUSE - DAY

Arrests being made. Riot cuffs. Minor punching and kicking by police. Routine noises of police radios. People are mostly on floor. In one corner, shaking with fright, A CRACKHEAD GIRL - who weighs under 100 pounds.

CUT TO:

INT POLICE PRECINCT - DAY

People are in holding cells being processed, fingerprinted, etc. Camera focusses in on Crackhead Girl - rail thin - looking very disoriented.

CUT TO:

INT. HOLDING CELL - DAY

Cold metal benches welded to the floor and walls. She is shivering. He yells. Somebody brings her a blanket.

CUT TO:

INT DRUG REHAB - DAY

Ruppert is standing in front of RECEPTIONIST/ SOCIAL WORKER's desk. Social Worker points to a waiting list that is totally full. Shakes her head.

END OF SEQUENCE

CUT TO:

RUPPERT'S STORY/CRUSH'S ROOTS

RUPPERT STARTS SEARCH FOR VERIFIABLE EVIDENCE OF DRUG DEALING.

ESTABLISHING CRUSH – MEETING THE NORIEGAS (USE STOCK FOOTAGE FROM SOME TV STATION - HERE OR IN PANAMA)

(waving boxes with arrows pointing at: "President of Panama" & "President of US.")

MEETING THE BIN LADENS - SAME BOXES - THERE IS A PHOTO - BOX READS "OSAMA BIN LADEN GRADUATING FORT BENNING"

CUT TO:

PLANES FLYING ALL OVER TEXAS AND MEXICO

MUSIC: BTO – "TAKING CARE OF BUSINESS"

INT. PROFESSOR'S CLASSROOM – DAY

In the background, Bachman Turner Overdrive – "Taking Care of Business" is warming up the background like a freight train picking up steam with shots of planes taking off and landing on dirt airstrips in Costa Rica then taking off to land again on military bases in the US. This time the "classroom" (which changes each time you see him) is an air traffic control tower with radar blipping in the background. The Professor in his white lab coat, carries a clipboard.
Music continues full volume ONLY DURING shots of Cessna and C-130 aircraft that are cut in (with SUBTITLES) between the shots of the Professor speaking to the class. When the professor is talking the music is low volume.

PROFESSOR
OK, so the question we have in front of us is: Is it a War on Drugs or is it a War (pause) *on* Drugs?

CUT TO:

C-130 taking off -- SUBTITLE: "CALI, COLUMBIA"

PROFESSOR (CONT)
What kind of drugs are they on?
TERESA,
(the cheerleader with a ponytail raises her hand:)
Cocaine?

CUT TO:

C-130 Landing -- SUBTITLE: "JOHN HULL'S RANCH - COSTA RICA"

CUT TO C-130 taking off again with SAME SUBTITLE

BONANZA

PROFESSOR
Very good, Teresa, and what else?

FRANCOIS
(with a heavy French accent)
Heroine?

CUT TO C-130 landing and taking off again

SUBTITLE: "ILOPANGO, EL SALVADOR"

PROFESSOR
Excellent, Francois, exactement.
And Teresa can you tell me why cocaine?

TERESA
Cocaine is a highly concentrated form of the coca leaf over 1000 times as powerful, and it makes the soldier incredibly alert and intense, ready for protracted action in the cockpit that can sometimes last for hours and hours.

PROFESSOR
And are there any negative effects?

TERESA
(in her best Valley Girl accent)
Well, yeah, of course, I mean, later, you know?

CUT TO CESSNA taking off SUBTITLE: "JOHN HULL'S RANCH - COSTA RICA"

PROFESSOR
And Francois, why Heroin for the combat soldier?

FRANCOIS
(intones in a thick French accent)
H'eroine is for to put the soldier calm and to sleep after he has been shot. It has a deep sedative effect, killing ze pain and also

creating a man who is almost incapable of complaining about anything. If the soldier comes to disagree with the war being fought, then it is much more manageable to have him angry from a deep sleep, no, instead of a high energy bursting, yes?

PROFESSOR
Yes, Francois, that is true.

CUT TO C-130 Landing in US in an Air Force Base surrounded by military aircraft

SUBTITLE: "UNDISCLOSED LOCATION, UNITED STATES"

VOICE OVER OF AIR TRAFFIC CONTROL TOWER:
Roger, you are 5 by 5 cleared for landing.

PILOT'S VOICE
Roger that.

CUT TO:

PROFESSOR
(Turns to a third student)
Yes, Pedro?

PEDRO
What about Crystal Meth, man? Why Crystal Meth?

PROFESSOR
We're not there yet, Pedro. This is still the 80's remember?

PEDRO
Oh, yeah, I forgot again, I always want to be ahead of my time, you know?

PROFESSOR
OK, class, study what you have just learned. It's very important that you understand these concepts when we move on to the Noriega Family and the Crushes connection to them and the

BuShiDo

Bin Laden Oil Empire.

PEDRO

But professor, this is the 80's, how do you know all this?

PROFESSOR

I read Mexican newspapers, Pedro.

PEDRO

Mexican newspapers?

PROFESSOR

They know things, Pedro.

PEDRO

They do? Like what things?

CUT TO one more C-130 landing.

MUSIC CRESCENDOS TO A RUSHING SOUND OF A JET ENGINE, THAT CHANGES SUDDENLY TO THE CRACK OF A BASEBALL BAT (MATCH ON ACTION TO SALVADOR YOU HITTING THE PLANE!)

CUT TO:

HASENFUS SHOT DOWN

SUB-TITLE: NICARAGUA OCTOBER 5TH, 1986

A field that looks very similar to the one where Young Salvador hit the home run in the opening scenes. Boys are playing baseball in the background and KID #2 at bat says:

KID #2

Dale, ya! (do it already!)

In the distance, a cargo plane is heard and moves over center field. As all the kids turn to watch it, a kid in military fatigues comes running up. All the kids turn to him and stare. He has a shoulder mounted anti-aircraft bazooka, he lines up the sites and shoots: WHOOSH!

The planes engines start to falter and then smoke starts to pour out of it as parachutes are seen opening.

PLANE CRASHES - LARGE FIREBALL.

KIDS
You hitting the plane! You hitting the plane!
(match on action to Young Salvador's at bat in first scene)

CUT TO:

INT. – NICARAGUAN LIVING ROOM – DAY

A bunch of FAT OLD MEN sit in a living room, drinking beer, watching a soccer game, and yelling at the set. Suddenly, the announcer gets on the TV. (in Spanish w/ subtitles) "We interrupt this program to bring you a special news brief"

(NOTE: Spanish to English translation on p.215-217)

NICARAGUAN REPORTER
Estamos aqui en Bosque del Campo donde ya mismito bajaron un avion EstadoUnidense Militar – no estan seguros pero parece a unos los misiones de narcotraficante de la policia secreto nominado la CIA. Y aqui estamos con Demetrio Macias, un chamaco de 15 anyos, que hace solo una hora atras, le tumbo al avion usando solo una bazooka de mano. !Que tiro, joven! ?Como tu te sientes?

KID WHO SHOT DOWN HASENFUS
(Eyes shiny with happiness, surrounded by cheering fans, family, girlfriend)
Muy bien, gracias a Dios, siempre he tenido esperanzas hacer algo para defender al pais de los gringos mataderos, pero nunca tuve ni un suenyo asi!

REPORTER

Mira este joven y que hizo con una arma sin radar sin nada. Impresionante, no. Y aqui que tenemos? Mira Senyor, escuse me sir, what are you doing here, mayn, hey, eco-tourism? You coming to study the plant life here? What is your problem coming over here, you got no right to fly you military planes anyplace you feel, no? You getting lost in Texas and you fly 2000 miles away from you forest fire? That's what you telling me this is – a forest fire fighter plane to spray the water, right? Wh'appen mayn? My English too fast for you? You speak a some Spanish I bet no? Yes you look no so much like a forest fireman who get lost. Here you wan' my cell phone so you can call them and then we can ask you Uncle what you doing flying over our country talking some story when you looking so much like a drug dealer even my grandmother can see who you is? Here take it my cell phone and call you Uncle Sam, tell him you need some lawyer, guns and money cause you get hit by a kid with a sling shot in you 20 million dollar plane OK? Here come on take it.

HASENFUS

(looks dazed but takes the phone, starts dialing but can't remember all the numbers.)

REPORTER

Man you no looking so good. (yells) Hey Chuchi! (whistles) Dale un poquito de agua. (to Hasenfus) Here sweetheart, lemme see the phone OK?

(Close Up Hasenfus. Hands Reporter the phone back. From off-screen big bucket of water is thrown on him.)

HASENFUS

Hey!!! Wait whoa, hey wait, what... wha.....um .....ohhh... (slumps again into daze looking off into the unfocussed distance)

REPORTER

Esweetheart, you in a bad, bad shape.

CUT TO:

EXT - A BEACH HUT IN COSTA RICA - SUNSET

MUSIC: "IT'S ALL RIGHT, HAVE A GOOD TIME, CAUSE IT'S ALL RIGHT..." is playing on the radio - not loud, but clearly audible both on their boom box and some other system you can't see.

Oliver North is smoking a joint w/ Fawn Hall. They are laying back on 2 beach recliners with little folding green canvas tables on either side of them. The mood is intimate. There are beers in a cooler on the sand, and some shrimp cocktail (ceviche) in plastic cups on ice. During most of this scene you are looking at them from the point of view of the Ocean.

FAWN HALL
(pointing at North:) Was Caesar following Robert's Rules of Order? Was Cleopatra? Huh? Vini, Vidi, Vici, Law of the Jungle, and really law of the land. Nature's law! No way around it. Never has been.

OLIVER NORTH
You wanna hear a good joke?

FAWN HALL
Yeah, tell me.

OLIVER NORTH
What's a hundred lawyers at the bottom of the ocean?

FAWN HALL
What?

OLIVER NORTH
(a grin spreads accross his face)
A good start.
(grin turns to a kind of poker face - like he don't think it's funny but he does)

FAWN HALL
(pauses, cocks her head to one side, looking at him with a sudden renewed affection)
You know you are so cute sometimes.

OLIVER NORTH
(smile comes back)
Cute? At the bottom of the ocean is cute?

FAWN HALL
No. - I meant it like you're adorable - and - I don't know - something else - it's like you're noble - not blue blood like all those politicians telling you what they want done and running like cowards every time some bureaucrat raises his hand in Congress. You don't run. You're noble like an animal -

OLIVER NORTH
- Baby, you think I'm an animal?

FAWN HALL
(stretching out her neck to kiss his shoulder, then his neck)
"Yesssss.... you are a live, ...powerful, ...fascinating .... animal. When you walk onto an airstrip in the middle of the jungle, I feel it - everybody does. People react instinctively to you. Like you or hate you, when you walk in a room - everybody pays attention - they respect you. In Washington, they all hide behind you - all the kiss-ass career politicians. They use you.
(She takes a swig of beer)
And all those asshole New York liberals who want to pretend like they were born in a small village in Honduras or some nonsense - acting like they didn't go to boarding school, and like somebody other than their mother elected them to be the voice of "El Pueblo Unido" - all those assholes hamstringing us with their little procedural details out of the Harvard Law Review - you know what? - not that we could do it - but if all of them ended up at the bottom of the ocean - nobody'd miss 'em really. Nobody real."

OLIVER NORTH
(raises his beer)
A toast.

FAWN HALL
To what?

OLIVER NORTH
To the American Sand Bar Association.

FAWN HALL
(clinking bottles with North)
Exactly.

CAMERA:
Slowly, from the ocean side, the camera pulls back and upwards, moving out over the water, showing the waves hitting the shore (momentarily drowning out the music). 2 Jeeps and a Humvee under camouflage netting appear parked under trees where the jungle meets the beach. There are tents, field radio units with long antennas, and a couple of soldiers making dinner. The camera skims over the waves and then pulls higher and higher. The music rises in volume ("It's all right, Have a good time, cause it's all right - Yeah, it's all right...") as the camera rises higher to skim over the top of a PT Boat sitting anchored off the coast. The music is coming from the boat's PA system, and you see a few soldiers on deck playing with automatic weapons slung over their shoulders. The camera rises sharply now. You see the jungle stretching out behind the beach to foothills. A helicopter suddenly jets in under the camera and heads into the interior at full speed. In seconds the helicopter is a speck - moving surprisingly fast almost like a jet fighter. Music comes back, but as the camera rises the Ocean reasserts its dominance. The shoreline fills the camera, jungle stretching out to the foothills and then mountains - higher still the camera floats like a rising balloon over the Caribbean, and the Mountains you see the Pacific Ocean where the sun will rise - without a doubt - tomorrow....

CUT TO:

INT. - SENATE IRAN-CONTRA HEARINGS - DAY

SUBTITLE: "SENATE HEARINGS ON THE IRAN-CONTRA AFFAIR"

SUBTITLE: "SENATOR DANIEL K. INOUYE - D - HAWAII"

SENATOR INOUYE

This hearing is now in closed session! No cameras, tape recorders, pagers, cellular phones, or other such devices will be permitted!

SHOT OF GAVEL SLAMMING ON DESK WITH SAME SOUND AS BASEBALL BAT.

CUT TO:

ONE HOUR TURNING POINT – DJ WANTS TO KNOW THE BARBERSHOP ANALYSIS:

Frustrated by all this swirling mass of conflicting information, Cassius Timmons takes some time off and goes back to his old neighborhood in East LA, where people have know him all his life. He walks down a familiar sidewalk, greets a couple of people with a nod and a handshake, and then comes to where he was headed, a small shoe shine stand on a corner near his old barbershop. Standing there as calm as if he was carved out of ebony, stands POPPA ZEE a man who has been like a second father to Cassius and explained a lot about life to the son of a Baptist Minister that Reverend Timmons would not or could not.

POPPA ZEE

Well, now, here we go, here we go. (breaks into a broad smile recognizing his favorite "nephew") Young man, it is a good thing to see you here this fine day! How are you Mr. DJ?

DJ

Jus' fine, Poppa Zee, doing just fine. How are you doing, sir?

POPPA ZEE

(reaching over to shake hands with DJ)

Can't complain and I wouldn't if I could.

DJ

I heard that. How's Auntie Tilly and them? I heard they had to move.

POPPA ZEE
(holding onto the 2 ends of a towel draped around his neck)
Oh, yes lord, they went and put in all that mess over there – that urban renewal crap – whole lotta Starbuck and Frappuccino mess and that health food store that don't know collards and chitlins from a hole in they backside. Talking all that good stuff about making things better over here and then don't go and hire but 2 people from the whole neighborhood. What a damn shame! Movin' all them people out they way like they was just visiting and going to tell us it's so we can get jobs, and they ain't hire but 2 people. Ain't that some mess?

DJ
(his forehead wrinkled in concern)
How many houses they knocked down?

POPPA ZEE
'Bout 4 or 5. The Connors, the Thomases used to be livin' over on Jefferson, and 3 other families moved here after you left. But it ain't really about that. I mean they paid pretty good money for them houses, but now we got all these people coming up in the neighborhood acting all goofy wandering around here like it Disneyland asking all type a stupid questions, now they wanting to buy up the houses, you know, make em look good for the gentry, you know? The elites is coming on in looking hungry, man, like they ain't been fed in weeks, man. Gotta laptop and one of them frappuccinos in a stainless steel cup look like it bulletproof. One a them Kevlar Cappuccinos, you know? But so far they's kind a shy about coming to get a shoe shine or a haircut or some fried Chicken over at Bessie's. Same old story, want to move in the neighborhood but don't want to talk to nobody. But Tilly and them is all right. She got a nice place over to Oak Street, corner a Maple. You should go see her, it would light up her day to see you come over and see her, just light up her day.

DJ
I'm a do that. Listen, Poppa Zee, this ain't exactly a social call –

POPPA ZEE
(concern rising in his voice)
What's wrong boy? You got troubles? –

DJ
No no nothing like that. I got questions.

POPPA ZEE
(leaning back on his heels, smiling, proud that his "nephew" still has need of his advice)
Boy, you always got some kind a question. Too damn nosy for your own good if you ask me. That's the question you should be asking is "Am I too damn nosy for my own good?"

DJ
(waving away the distraction)
OK, OK I got that, but that's how I am and somebody asked a question the other day that really has me wondering about a lot of things.

POPPA ZEE
(settling in to listening mode)
What was the question?

DJ
They wanted to know if the Crush Family if they like a mafia family, you know? Like if they selling drugs and stuff like the Italians got their families, you know like the Gottis or that kind of thing. They're saying that Crush was selling drugs all the way back to the Viet Nam days.

POPPA ZEE
(eyes open wide like someone just hit him)
Hold - up - a – minute! Dear lord Jesus Why you gotta send all the crazy kids to my block? First you gotta send me the kids that don't know how to do right, and if that ain't enough now you gotta take the ones that's knowing how to do right and got them looking for all kind a mess to mess with that ain't even they mess! Lord have mercy! (all serious) Cassius do you have a cell phone?

DJ
Yeah you need to call someone?

POPPA ZEE
(imitating) Do I need to call someone! Give it here!

DJ
(handing over the phone)
OK.

(Poppa Zee takes out a bag of Doritos and spills out all the chips and stuffs the phone in the bag)

DJ (CONT'D)
What the hell - ?

POPPA ZEE
I seen it in a movie, now give me your shoes, your watch and your fountain pen.

DJ
What? Stop playing.

POPPA ZEE
(laughing takes the cell phone out the bag)
All right but hold on a minute. (takes the cell phone and pulls out the battery.)

DJ
What you take my battery for?

POPPA ZEE
Never you mind, - just say I don't like two way radios in my private conversations. How long you known me?

DJ
All my life.

POPPA ZEE
And how long you been seeing me holding down not one but two families shining shoes every day?

DJ
All my life.

POPPA ZEE
Now you was asking me another in a long running set of episodes of dumb-ass questions about stuff that don't concern you. Right?

DJ
It does concern –

POPPA ZEE
Why child? Why do this crazy bullshit concern you? Why do people in far away places with they own craziness coming down for God knows how long, why do you gotta go make all that your business?

DJ
(getting mad)
Because of Cassie, goddammit! Because of Cassie! You know it well as I do, now. When she died it broke Momma's heart – she ain't never been the same since. And Daddy still ain't forgive himself, and he never will, and neither will I. That's why!

POPPA ZEE
(voice somber)
She was a beautiful child.... So full of life.
(silence falls for a moment)
Cassius, knowing it was the Italians or the Russians or the Gottis or any of them – it ain't gonna bring her back. It ain't. Son, I did the best I could to show you and the other boys out here your way around in the world, you know, how it work, and how to make your way and how to keep from getting the man from letting you live your life. And that is my advice to you son. Live your life! You doing fine. You making us all proud and you

doing the right things. You setting an example for all these kids out here to see. Can't you see how valuable that is? Why you want to go charging off on some crusade, stirring up trouble that ain't come looking for you?

DJ

(pounding his fist into his open hand)

But Poppa, it did come looking for me. It came looking for everybody I know. You know what this neighborhood was like before the Crack epidemic. You old enough to remember the changes that came down like a ton of bricks on every single neighborhood in this city. It ain't used to be like this. Even if you was poor, it wasn't like this, and you know that!

POPPA ZEE

Those was different times son. Those was different times. It was nice being able to trust people some. It was a good way to live. But you can't fight city hall, Cassius. You can duck it, you can shuck it, you can jive it, but you really can't fight it.

DJ

(measuring his words carefully for full effect)

Look - I know you, and I respect you. I respect your ways and your wisdom. But you know me. You know once I get it in my head to know about something I am not going to stop until I get it right. True or not? (Poppa Zee nods, sighs) And that is the only way I know how to be. And that is what makes me who I am – you say you proud of me – well, OK, that's who you proud of. Someone with no sense of when to let well enough alone. Not on this. If the government was in on this making deals and flying planes and setting up Noriega and them and taking a cut of the profits then that makes the Tuskeegee Experiments look like kid stuff. Now I'm hearing a whole bunch of stuff, and I need somebody to give me the breakdown, cause like I said people is saying all kind of stuff. And some of it making sense and some of it just sound like they angry at the world and thinking like Crush is an alien, and he responsible for everything that ever went wrong in the world.

POPPA ZEE
(shaking his head)
Boy, you like a pit bull you know that? Get your jaw locked on something and can't let go no matter if it's a bull elephant. But for all your stubbornness, you sure is one blind kind a pit bull. Just remember what I told you, all this knowledge about current events and world history, it ain't gonna do you a bit a good – not one bit

DJ
Please Poppa Zee, I just gotta know

MUSIC "WHEN DID CRACK HIT?" - JUNGLE BROTHERS AND KRS (Who was in office?)

RUPPERT MEETS WITH DJ FOR FIRST TIME

EXT. – LA BURRITO SHACK – DAY

DJ
So then when did Crush start importing?

RUPPERT
At least back in Viet Nam.

DJ
So you mean like the late 60's?

RUPPERT
No no, man. Viet Nam was a war all the way back in the 1920's. The French had Viet Nam. It was their colony, just like the British had America. You remember the movie "The French Connection?" That was about heroin that the French were bringing over from their Colony which was Viet Nam.

DJ
OK, fine but you still didn't answer my question about when Crush started moving drugs.

RUPPERT
1954.

DJ
That early?

RUPPERT
At least. We started backing the French when they started losing the war around 1948, but in 1954 the US basically bought the rights to Viet Nam.

DJ
What do you mean, bought the rights?

RUPPERT
We bought the contract. We took over the colony. Viet Nam was too much for France to handle after World War 2. So we bought the colony, and with the colony came the rights to its biggest cash crop.

DJ
Heroin?

RUPPERT
It wasn't rice cakes.

CUT TO:

SOMETHING ABOUT JERICHO (A Dramatization)

EXT - REFLECTING POOL BY THE LINCON MEMORIAL (1998) - DAY

BILLY BOB and BUBBA were out fishing down by the reflecting pool one day in 1998...

BUBBA
Eh Billy Bob!

BILLY BOB
Yeah Bubba

BUBBA:
I was down over to the Arabian Pizza & Espresso Shop the other day talking to one of the Bin Laden boys -

BILLY BOB:
They really such a thing as Arabian Pizza and Espresso, Bubba?

BUBBA:
Oh yeah, they was making pizza & espresso before Rome was built by them Wolf Boys Masonry and Contracting outfit.

BILLY BOB:
Arabians?

BUBBA:
All them Mess - a - Potamians.

BILLY BOB:
Oh yeah that is true. So what did Fidel - I mean Pol Pot - I mean Abdul have to say?

BUBBA:
Bin Laden.

BILLY BOB:
Whatever.

BUBBA:
See, that's why I can't talk to you about important matters - you're blind to the fundamentals a the game.

BILLY BOB:
Justice is blind, Bubba. I just don't give a fuck. There's a difference.

BUBBA:
Well lemme just remind your pork barrel ass that playing stupid don't make you smart.

BILLY BOB:
Listen here Professor Xavier, why don't you just skip the philosophy, and get to the point?

BUBBA:
Fuck you, Billy.

BILLY BOB:
Fuck you too, Bubba. Now what's the point? Time is money.

BUBBA:
One of the bin Ladens from Saudi Arabia -

BILLY BOB:
They all bin Ladens over in that country - must be like 10 fractions all kind of weird associations, and every one of em it's either a bin Laden or a bin Mafouz running it. Whatever crazy flavor of Abdul a bin Mafouz is.

BUBBA:
Bin Mafouz started the bank that Islamic law says you can't have.

BILLY BOB:
They say you can't have banks?

BUBBA:
Yupper.

BILLY BOB:
Hey maybe Islam ain't so bad after all.

BUBBA:
You know, Bobby, some of em is just like Buffalo Soldiers with straight hair and others of them actually is more like Country

Club Cowboys from Houston.

BILLY BOB:
You don't say?

BUBBA:
I do.

BILLY BOB:
So OK what flavor was we talking about here at the Arabian Pizza Shop?

BUBBA:
Now Billy I wouldn't want you gettin' all confused about something as simple as a Pol Pot lovin', Houkah smokin' Abdul...

BILLY BOB:
Naw, Bubba, I know what a Country Club Cowboy is even if he do got a tan, and I never heard of no Rastafarian Towel Heads, but I do get around.

BUBBA:
That so Billy?

BILLY BOB:
Fuck you, Bubba.

BUBBA:
Fuck you too, Billy Bob. Now could you tell me precisely what kind of inbred baby food I'm supposed to feed you to instantly enlighten you as to who we're talking about getting in on a 30 year non-negotiable mortgage with? (pauses)
First off, Mo-Ron, Buffalo Soldiers wasn't no Bob Marley with Dread Locks - they was Union Soldiers just freed from Slavery with regulation crew cuts what fought the Indians up and down the desert and helped to make the Great State of Texas. The Indians called them Buffalos cause they could move over hard desert country. They had great endurance and the

Indians respected that even while they hated them - so that and the black curly hair reminded them of the Buffalo. Danny Glover made the movie, but Colin Powell could tell you a thing or two about Buffalo Soldiering.

BILLY BOB:
OK, but so what flavor of Arab is talking to you about which kind of Pizza? Get to the damn point.

BUBBA:
Basically, a set of the Houston kind of Saudis - mixed bunch actually - is talking about a land deal they got going in the Middle East all on out to China.

BILLY BOB:
Central Asia?

BUBBA:
Yupper.

BILLY BOB
Expensive real estate.

BUBBA
Yupper.

BILLY BOB:
OK .... And this is our deal or their deal or whose deal?

BUBBA:
You know what they say - no point owning everything in a company worth nothing.

BILLY BOB:
OK but what company? Whose on the Board of Directors?

BUBBA:
Well on our side, this is mostly a Halliburton/Carlysle Group deal.

BILLY BOB:
O - K and Crush is signed on for promo?

BUBBA:
Full Radio and TV blitz - War on Terror, Stop Saddam, looking for bin Laden's secret bases, the whole 9.

BILLY BOB:
But - uh - Bubba, first are you talking Osama bin Laden, the Afghanistan Freedom Fighter? What secret bases? I thought those were our bases...

BUBBA:
See, Billy, this is where it pays to pay attention. Osama is a Saudi Arabian Prince turned Country Club Cowboy who became an overnight general working against Russia using American weapons, and -

BILLY BOB:
- It pays to pay attention, Bubba, when I see Black Gold - up til then it's all speculation. Crush in the White House is still speculation.

BUBBA:
That's true, Billy. But I got a friend over at Dieboldt knows more about fixing a fight than Don King.

BILLY BOB:
What's Dieboldt again?

BUBBA:
Voting machines, my illiterate son, electronic ATM style voting machines with no paper trail.

BILLY BOB:
No recountable record?

BUBBA:
Your word against mine. And we, my friend - we got the computer's password in our back pocket.

BILLY BOB:
That ain't - no Democrat in the World is gon' let that go.

BUBBA:
Billy, my naïve son, what is the ruling party of the Great City of Chicago? And how corrupt are their elections?

BILLY BOB:
I know all that - but no paper ballots?

BUBBA:
No paper ballots.

BILLY BOB:
Electronic vote counts?

BUBBA:
Ee - Lec - Tronic.

BILLY BOB:
OK, so you got a Halliburton/Carlysle Production with a promo package and some kind of Saudis looking for Central Asia, and who else is on the team?

BUBBA:
Well, England.

BILLY BOB:
Yeah.

BUBBA:
And West Germany.

BILLY BOB:
OK.

BUBBA:
And I think Israel.

BILLY BOB:
Israel?!! Israel and West Germany?!!!

BUBBA:
Yupper.

BILLY BOB:
Israel and Saudi Arabia and West Germany together on a land deal?

BUBBA:
You'd be surprised how money can ease you past religious differences.

BILLY BOB:
(quoting)
"No Atheists in foxholes..."

TOGETHER:
"And no Bankers neither."

BILLY BOB:
OK so but what are the teams?

BUBBA:
Basically US and Western Europe vs. China.

BILLY BOB:
But what about Saudi Arabia and Israel?

BUBBA:
OK on the local sides its Israel and Saudi Arabia vs. Iran & Iraq & Afghanistan.

BILLY BOB:
But Iran & Iraq don't get along so good remembering the 80's.

BUBBA:
That makes it easier for us.

BILLY BOB:
True enough. What about Eastern Europe?

BUBBA:
Who cares? They're so deep in debt, even Russia's on sale 10 cents on the dollar.

BILLY BOB:
Still a big army.

BUBBA:
True, but the smart money is on them standing pat for this one.

BILLY BOB:
Canada and Mexico?

BUBBA:
Canada been more French than France since for as long as I can remember - too busy making cheese and trees and free pills for the masses - sides they probably still flying P-51 Mustangs.

BILLY BOB:
And Mexico?

BUBBA:
Well, way I figure it, that's a lot of manpower looking for a green card. You could trade green cards for draft cards and come up with a couple of divisions.

BILLY BOB:
And what about them? What do they want?

BUBBA:
Them who?

BILLY BOB:
The locals - the Central Asians - I mean the Kurds and the

Shi-ites and the Pakistans and all of 'em. Who do they want running the show?

BUBBA:
Billy, beggars can't be choosers.

BILLY BOB:
Bubba, you mean to say - seriously - that this don't concern you in the least regarding states rights?

BUBBA:
Oh shit, Billy, that old saw don't apply! It ain't relevant, and I wish you wouldn't keep bringing it up.

BILLY BOB:
Damn it, Bubba, we can't go pissing on people every damn place and call it exporting democracy forever. That ain't worth all the tea in China or Boston - and if you ain't noticed there's been an increase in the number of Boston Tea Parties lately.

BUBBA:
Billy, you're looking at people who wouldn't know democracy if it landed on em like a pair of 500 pound bombs - all these people know is fighting.

BILLY BOB:
You mean like the Democrats and Republicans getting so far up my ass, I can't build a treehouse in my own backyard without a building permit while Wal-Mart practically gets paid to put in a new mega mall while clerks bend over backwards and fill all the paperwork out and mail it to them V.I.P. - those kine a 500 pound bombs?

BUBBA:
OK Billy, you want the big picture? You got the Kurds half in Iraq half in Turkey, half in Iran who don't like the Shi-ites who don't like the Sunnis who mostly all don't like Saddam, and all of em got reasons going back to the Old Testament, which if you ain't up on your Sunday School is bee - fore the New Testament which was when they came up with the word BC, so the family arguments go back a few thousand years, and they got all our oil.

BILLY BOB:
I thought the Arabians got all our oil?

BUBBA:
That's why we're not fighting the Arabians - we're fighting who they tell us to fight.

BILLY BOB:
What about the Russian and Canadian Oil?

BUBBA:
I told you: It's easier to get Mid-East Oil than Canadian Oil.

BILLY BOB:
How is this easier?
I don't like it. Those people got a delicate Hatfield-McCoy relationship, and we went and installed Saddam and messed it all up, and so now we gotta uninstall Saddam, and we been at it since '91, and everybody's just draggin' their feet like they enjoying the Chaos and meantime we got a Country Club Cowboy from Saudi Arabia installed in Afghanistan and messing their ecosystem up and meantime I'm a tell you one thing - American Weapons or not - those Afghanistan Mountain Men opened up a serious can of whoop-ass on our behalf and did us a great favor in the Cold War beating Russia like that and now we gon turn around and take their country, and mountain men don't forget that kind a crap - they don't - ain't no amount a money gon' change how they lookin at you - that war with Russia lasted 10 long years - that ain't no walk in the park.

BUBBA:
Do you want in on this or not?

BILLY BOB:
For a Professor Xavier you don't listen too good. When is this here Lupay Fiasco suppose to start?

BUBBA:
'Bout 2002 - Right after the little surprise.

BILLY BOB:
What little surprise?

BUBBA:
That, my boy, is super deluxe for me to know and you to watch out for...

BILLY BOB:
You ever heard of throwing good money after bad?

BUBBA:
And?

BILLY BOB:
This is the same thing only with blood thrown in for good measure. We're throwing good innocent blood after bad. And it's the young kids in school now that are going to pay for every bit of blood money we're spending like idiots with credit cards - that's my word on the subject - that's my word.

BUBBA:
Your word?

BILLY BOB:
Just like Kidd Rock says.

CUT TO:

MUSIC: ODB - "Ghetto Superstar"
"My eyes is sore from being a Senator...the rich going off ignore the tug of war while the kids are poor up in Newark by the Drug Stores, so I became hard core, couldn't take it no more...gon' reveal everything, change the law . I find myself walking the streets, trying to find out what's really going on in the streets..."

Rest in Peace

"Soon I will be the man, I'm supposed to be." - Toots (Maytals) - What a Bam Bam

"Isn't it a shame to spend your life away like this?" - James Marshall Hendryx - I don't live today

RETURNING TO CONVERSATION DJ AND RUPPERT BY TACO STAND:

EXT. – LA TACO STAND – DAY

RUPPERT
(pulls out book, "Cocaine Politics" by Peter Dale Scott, and slaps it down on the table)
There!

DJ
What's that?

RUPPERT
That, my son, is required reading.

DJ
What do you mean, required reading?

RUPPERT
Well, respectfully, you're about to ask me a whole set of difficult to answer questions, right? You suddenly got a burning desire to know and somebody told you I'm some kind of Top Secret expert with some sort of dark past, who's been doing undercover work for the quote "shadow government" and now I've decided to go AWOL and reveal my secrets to the highest bidder, right?

DJ
Whatever.

RUPPERT
Except when all is said and done you got a 2 second attention

span, plus you got no money for me and on top of it all it's 50/50 by the end of our conversation you're gonna haul off for no reason and call me a wacko instead of thanking me for taking the time to try to answer your questions politely and calmly.

DJ

What's your point?

RUPPERT

You're going to ask me a bunch of questions, BUT you're probably not going to believe the answers I'm going to give you because there's no hard evidence. So BEFORE we go there, and I get pissed off about it, this book is your hard evidence, and plenty of it.

I'm not saying that it's going to happen, but it has happened before. People ask me what I know, I tell them, and they turn around and go "Bullshit, you're just a beat cop. How are you gonna know all that?"

DJ

OK so for instance say that's what I'm thinking. What's the book for?

RUPPERT

Like I said: Required Reading.

That's the story of the Christic Institute – a non profit group of Church going lawyers and priests and legislators. They brought a lawsuit against the government in 1986, saying a lot of the same things I found out the hard way.

I am giving you the benefit of 20 years experience as a police officer and it doesn't cost you a thin dime, BUT. What you don't pay me in money, you are going to pay me in respect. This is my life. As you brothers like to say, "The shit is Real." Do we understand eachother?

DJ

Don't go popping some Ying-Yang bullshit on me, just cause I'm black. I hear you, and I respect you, OK? But you better understand respect is a 2 way street. You got to give it to get it. Jus' so you know, my father is a deacon in the First Baptist Church downtown, and I did a tour of duty with an honorable discharge. Feel me, homey? (last sentence is thick with barely suppressed anger at the comment about "The shit is real.")

RETURN TO POPPA ZEE AND DJ:

EXT. – SHOE SHINE STAND – EAST LOS ANGELES

POPPA ZEE

Now LA gangs wasn't really nothing before about 1945 to 50. Even then they wasn't much. Now drugs was coming in the country way before then. Cocaine was actually something the Germans had got into back before the turn of the century. And it didn't hit LA til about 1910 or so. Matter of fact, Coca-Cola got its name cause it was made with Cocaine. And they was feeding it to kids without those kids knowing. All they knew was it made them jump around.

Now back then, if you was going to buy a kilo of Coke you couldn't go to the Mexicans. Mexicans was only into weed, and it was that old school weed. Naw, man, if you wanted Coke and Heroin you was dealing with white people. The French was bringing Heroin over from Viet Nam – they called it French Indochina back then. Or you was dealing with the Italians. Or maybe some of them was dealing with the Germans direct. It was the Germans that made the first Cocaine quiet as kept. Wasn't no Mexicans big up in the Organized Crime thing. They was all Italians, or Irish or French or Chinese, and quiet as kept, the English – they was running Opium out of India. The English got as much Organized Crime in them as any of those Italians, trust. Back before they had all the Italians and the Irish gangs, the first gangs was English. That's how they took over America, cause they was ruthless. And what I told you about them running Opium out of India – that's true. You can even read it in the history books. See you gotta study crime close up, you want to see who's running things today. Same family running things turn of the century probably still in the same game today. The Kennedy's may come off all civilized but they a gangster family. Used to run whiskey and stuff all through the prohibition time. You scratch a Kennedy even now, you gonna see a gangster. They still roll that way. Now, what is that book you got there? (reads) "Co-Cayne Politics" Well that's two things that do go together. What's it say?

DJ

That Crush's family is like an American Mafia. That they running drugs out of Viet Nam and Laos, and Columbia and El Salvador, using the CIA for cover.

POPPA ZEE

Well, shoot, that's a mouthful.
So, but.... well ....hmmm.
Lemme see if I can make this as simple as possible for you. I mean what states do Crush Family control? Think about it.

DJ

Well, he got Texas, right?

POPPA ZEE

Yep, what else?

DJ

They seem to have a lock on Florida, too, remembering the last 2 elections, right?

POPPA ZEE

Oh yeah, Crush been strong in Florida for a long, long time.

DJ

And he's from Maine.

POPPA ZEE

Right, but what else, where else has Crush got?

DJ

Where?

POPPA ZEE
Right here. Cal-I-for-NI-ay.

DJ
Oh yeah.

POPPA ZEE
Remember Reagan?

DJ
Yup.

POPPA ZEE
How about Nixon?

DJ
True.

POPPA ZEE
And Crush was head of the CIA when Nixon was president. The Governator's not exactly a liberal either. Trust me Crush got his hands deep in Cali.

DJ
So?

POPPA ZEE
Young man too lazy. Want other people do all the thinking for 'em. Can't add 2 + 2 without a computer or a Ipod with a modem or some shit.

DJ
Look, Poppa Zee, what is your point?

POPPA ZEE
Boy, you slower than molasses on the misty mountain top! What did I just tell you?

DJ
Where Crush Family got its strongholds.

POPPA ZEE
Which is where?

DJ
(slowly)
Texas, right and California, and Florida.

POPPA ZEE
And what's in Florida?

DJ
Miami. So?

POPPA ZEE
So where do Crush Family control?

DJ
Texas, Cali, and Miami. So?

POPPA ZEE
Boy, where do all the drugs come into this country?!!!

DJ
(finally gets it)
Ohhh,......shiiiiiiit! (exhaling)

POPPA ZEE
(slowly, drawing it out)
Texas,... Miami,... and – Cali.

DJ
(repeating with growing resonance)
Texas, Miami, and Cali.

POPPA ZEE
Sing it with me!

BOTH (DJ AND POPPA ZEE)
Texas, Miami, and Cali! Texas, Miami, and Cali!
Texas, Miami and Cali!

POPPA ZEE
Sing!

BOTH (DJ AND POPPA ZEE)
Texas, Miami, and Cali! Texas, Miami, and Cali!
Texas, Miami and Cali!
(keep going, hopping around like kids who just discovered a new game to play)

KIDS look over – rolling their eyes – not knowing what has gotten into these two.

FADE OUT

("Where in the hell is Kennebunkport, Texas?")

MUSIC HERMANOS LEBRON – "AMAZONA"
b/w
MUSIC "TEXAS, MIAMI, AND CALI" - TBA

ERNESTO ARRIVES LA

ERNESTO
Hi, Am I on live radio?

DJ
You are live on the air. Who am I talking to?

ERNESTO
This is Ernesto. I am from El Salvador.

DJ
Yes, what can we do for you Ernesto from El Salvador.

ERNESTO
I am listening to you talking about the cocaine trafficking, and

BuShiDo

we in our country are suffering from the effects of the trade. They kill many people to establish a more strong cocaine trade connection through our country.

DJ

When you say “They”, who do you mean?

ERNESTO

The Secret Police.

DJ

(slowing down)

The Secret Police?

ERNESTO

Yes the Secret Police in our country is call La Guardia, and in your country is call La See-Ya.

DJ

(more skepticism)

The “See-Ya?”

KWAME

The C-I-A, Cassius, That’s how Spanish people pronounce it.

DJ

The CIA?

ERNESTO

Yess. The Secret Police in you country make a contract with the Secret Police in our country to use our airfield to land they military planes to refuel from Colombia and go to United States with cocaine.

DJ

You have proof of this?

ERNESTO

Yes.

DJ
Can you come to the radio station?

ERNESTO
Yes. If I can cross the border today. I will come tomorrow.

DJ
Cross the border? Where are you?

ERNESTO
Tijuana. I hear you on the radio station.

DJ
And you're legal to cross?

ERNESTO
Yes. I am enroll as a student in your UCLA to learn film make.

DJ
Film make?

ERNESTO
I want to make a movie about how the Marines kill my Tia the nun.

#3
Yo! This dude on crack! You ain't making no movie, son. No -- way. Period. End of Story.

ERNESTO
I am no on crack! I am telling you I have books from this!

DJ
But you got proof, right? CIA planes moving drugs?

ERNESTO
Yes. Everyone knows this where I am from. I will make it a movie.

#3
You ain't makin' no kine a damn movie!

ERNESTO
I am too going make it a movie!!!

DJ
WILL YOU TWO STOP?!!! For right now can we leave making a movie for later and just concentrate on getting you on the radio? Do you have this proof? And a student Visa?

ERNESTO
I have this proof. And a Visa.

DJ
Don't - Do Not - hang up. Somebody's going to give you directions, OK?

ERNESTO
OK.

CUT TO:

INT - RADIO STATION RECEPTION AREA - DAY

Ernesto opens door tentatively, not sure if he's in the right place. Walks over to desk.

ERNESTO
Excuse me, I am looking for Cassius Timmons.

DJ
(Looking up from where he is checking his mail)
Are you Ernesto?

ERNESTO
Yes, I am Ernesto. Who are you?

DJ
I'm the guy you talked to on the radio, Cassius Timmons, pleased to meet you. So you made it alright crossing the border?

ERNESTO
Yes. It took a long time but no problems.

DJ
(motioning for Ernesto to follow him)
Man, I am happy to meet you! Here come on into the conference room. Do you want something to drink?

ERNESTO
No, it's OK maybe in a minute.

CUT TO:

INT RADIO STATION CONFERENCE ROOM - DAY

Ernesto & the DJ sit down. Ernesto has his back pack out in front of him and proceeds to dump a whole set of books out on to the conference table including a couple of photo albums and a scrap book.

DJ
What's all this?

ERNESTO
You saying you want a proof, so I bring proof.

DJ
All this is proof?

ERNESTO
There a lot of proof. Lotta people see what happen.

DJ
All right, show me.

As Ernesto opens his scrap-book with photos and newspaper clippings, the camera cuts to full screen shots of the photos while Ernesto describes each one.

ERNESTO
This is my Tia, Esmerelda Jimenez-Sanchez in her high school. She was first going to be a Doctor, and then she join in the Church to become a nun. Later, during the time of Duarte, she was protesting that so many had been disappear by the Military Junta, but in this picture she about to start Medical School in San Salvador.

DJ
She was very beautiful.

ERNESTO
Thank you. Everybody say so. She was even more beautiful inside. She was my favorite.

DJ
So can I ask: What happened?

ERNESTO
(flipping pages in book to news clipping)
They kill her. The Secret Police take her and dump her body next to the road. (he gets quiet).

DJ
I'm sorry.

CUT TO:

CLOSE UP OF ERNESTO
(his face is suddenly resolved, hardened, like a different person residing behind the college student raised to be polite and well-mannered)
Don't be sorry. Make them sorry they did it.

DJ

(pausing, somewhat stunned - both by the sudden change in his expression and what he just said)
I don't know how I could do that.

ERNESTO

Tell the truth. They say they are Christians. Tell the truth about what they did. Killing old women to open up a highway so they could sell more drugs. Tell them that, show the hypocrisy, and you job is done.

DJ

OK, but you gotta give me the proof. I can't go into this thing half-stepping. I got my own reasons why I want to know. But you gotta give me the facts - cold, hard, facts. Not opinions, facts. Cause where we about to go, there's gonna be some major resistance, ya heard? Nobody wants to hear that the President of the United States is dealing drugs. Nobody.

ERNESTO

You want a proof? Get a pencil. Cause chances are you no going to get to see too many people from El Salvador with papers and an attitude like mine.

DJ

Oh you got a attitude? (smiling) Good. Me, too. Now, what is this book?

Camera pulls back to show the whole conference table as music (an instrumental version of Soul II Soul - "Keep on Moving") comes up and the conversation dissolves into bits and pieces as we cut from shot to shot of the DJ and Ernesto talking about the books, looking at photos from newspapers, waving and gesturing with their hands almost like they're arguing or debating.

MUSIC: KEEP ON MOVING - SOUL II SOUL (INSTR.)
(One reason is it's easy to lower volume and it isn't massive depression music.)

ERNESTO (Voice Over)
(as we see a full screen photo of Crush shaking hands with President Duarte.)
Mr. Crush always helping the worst dictators in Latin America. In El Salvador, Duarte and Medrano were known by everybody as very bad men, and Crush helped them with lots of money. He made them powerful.

DJ
And what's this?

ERNESTO
This is the amount of Cocaine imported into the US during when Crush was Vice President in charge of the Task Force for preventing Drugs.

DJ
It did go up.

ERNESTO
A lot.

DJ
Who's that?

ERNESTO
Generallisimo Senyor Presidente Manuel Noriega of Panama

DJ
That's Noriega?

ERNESTO
That's Noriega. And here he is with you President making international businesses.

DJ
And this was when the Cocaine Imports were going through the roof.

ERNESTO
Exactly.

DJ
What about this other book?...

scene fades:to blank white screen.

CUT TO

FLASHBACK: SOLDIERS KILLING TIA

EXT. RURAL EL SALVADOR – EVENING

Screen has a sort of hazy look almost out of focus - a dreamy quality. Sound is muted as well.

SUB-TITLE: "El Salvador 1984"

Soldiers in jeeps and on foot running down a hillside into a village past the town square with it's water cistern and small bandstand. They are shooting in the air - assault rifles, beating and driving people with the butts of their rifles. Animals (cows, donkeys, dogs) are running, barking, etc.
Close Up of soldiers kicking in the doors of several houses and pulling people out of the houses, and rounding them up into town square. More shots are fired. People, children are crying and screaming.

CUT TO:

INT, RURAL EL SALVADOR – CHURCH - EVENING

(NOTE: Spanish to English translation on p. 218)

SALVADOR'S TIA, a nun, is trying to make a phone call to get help. You hear the line go dead. She runs accross the room to the front door, frantic, throws her body into the weight of the heavy door, and bursts outside, shouting at the soldiers.

SALVADOR'S TIA
NO! NO HAN HECHO NADA! (NO! THEY HAVEN'T DONE ANYTHING!)

A soldier she is screaming at grunts, and knocks her out with the butt of his rifle.

CUT TO:

INT -CHURCH - RURAL EL SALVADOR - DAY

SALVADOR'S TIA is on the phone yelling at the official on the other end. She is wearing nun's habit and her head is bandaged.

SALVADOR'S TIA
?Pero, senyor, donde estan? Lo unico que quiero decir es que no son mala gente, y uno no se puede arrestar a la gente sin decir donde estan!

OFFICIAL
Eso es un asunto federal. Yo te consejo no ponerte en el medio de cosas que no pertenece a ti.

SALVADOR'S TIA
!Esos son mis vecinos! Mis hijos! ?Como que no pertenecen a mi?!!!

CUT TO:

INT- CHURCH - RURAL EL SALVADOR – NIGHT

Camera is focussed on the massive wooden doors. Suddenly there is a pounding - ONE - TWO - THREE TIMES - and soldiers burst through using a battering ram, they cross quickly and kick down the door to SALVADOR'S TIA' S room. Amid scuffling and muffled screams, she is bound, gagged, and dragged out to a waiting Armored Personnel Carrier where she is thrown in the back. They drive off.

CUT TO:

EXT - RURAL EL SALVADOR – DAY

News cameras are crowded around a ditch next to a road. The body of Salvador's Tia has been found, buried in a shallow grave by the side of the road. Her SISTER - Salvador's mother - is holding her to her breast, body wracked with sobs, as Salvador comes up and recognizing who it is, begins to wail uncontrollably.

A photographer comes up and snaps a photo which goes black and white and then pulls back to reveal the news story that goes with it - all of it pasted into one of the pages of Salvador's Scrap Book.

ERNESTO

The number one way the ruling families have of hiding the drug trade is to be like "Where are the dealers? I can't find them." They make up a story where the drug dealers are basically invisible. They pretend that all of the drugs are being moved by these heroes that never pay taxes and have no connections to the military or the government. They pretend that the majority of the weight move accross the borders is done by people like Pancho Villa and Che Guevara or rap stars like Mac-10 or Dr. Dre. They are making us believe that nobody in Organized Crime got anything to do with legitimate businesses or the military business.

DJ

The military industry?

ERNESTO

Companies that make the planes, helicopters, ships, submarines, weapons systems, the people that are the real killers in any society.

DJ

Yes, I understand you. You're really... something.

ERNESTO
Something like what?

DJ
I guess just really idealistic.

ERNESTO
Maybe. That's what everybody telling me. I don't think of myself that way.

DJ
How do you mean? How do you see yourself?

ERNESTO
I see things that happen, and I describe what is really happening. No the cover story, the real people involved in killing people. After what I see, this is what I know to do. It affect everybody different. This is how it affect me. I see them killing my Tia, an old woman, who don't hurt nobody. What would you do?

CUT TO:

MUSIC "JUST SOME GOOD OLE BOYS" - DUKES OF HAZZARD THEME

Take it easy. Every government lies more to the inside than to the outside.

INT. – DJ'S CAR – DAY

On the way to meet the ATTORNEY from the Christic Institute, Ruppert fills in the details on the basics of their case:

DJ
So who is this Christic Institute anyway?

RUPPERT
A group of radical lawyers.

DJ
So what exactly was their lawsuit about?

RUPPERT
This is the way it went:
We were supposedly fighting a war to stop drugs, right? There was a whole lot of money being spent by the Reagan/Crush Administrations for extra police and extra jails and extra helicopters and boats and planes and extra everything. The Christic Institute went to them with the names of major dealers – not mid-level guys – I mean heavy hitters, and they told them "Hey, here's your evidence, these are the guys and a lot of them are on the CIA's payroll, so if you want to reduce the imports of drugs it might be a good idea to stop paying the dealers' salaries and legal expenses."

DJ
OK, and then what?

RUPPERT
And the federal judges went out of their way to suppress the evidence. In all honesty the CIA had major drug dealers on the payroll, and the US Department of Justice was on the CIA's side. They did everything they could to squash the case before it could get any publicity. And really they did a pretty good job. I mean you never heard of the Christic Institute case of May 29,1986, right? That lawsuit is way bigger than Watergate, and in Watergate you are talking about several hundred thousand dollars being laundered. Maybe as much as 2 million dollars. In the Christic Institute case which is the real Iran Contra Investigation, the figures start at 2 million and move pretty fast up into the 200 million dollar range. And the judges threw the case out of court before the first evidence was even presented. Not only that, they fined the Christic Institute $1.5 million dollars.

DJ
Why?

RUPPERT
They said that the lawsuit was a waste of the taxpayers money. They pulled an obscure rule out of the books that says if a lawyer brings a quote frivolous lawsuit against the government – then the government can levy a fine as a penalty for wasting the judges time. How is it frivolous to point out that the US is allying itself with the largest drug dealers in Latin America? $1.5 million dollars! It was unbelievable. There was no precedent on the books for that kind of a fine. That fine is meant to be used as a slap on the wrist. They used that fine to knock the Christic Institute into bankruptcy for asking a question – for exercising their rights as US citizens to question the government in a court of law.

DJ
What does frivolous mean? – I know what it means – but what does it mean in legal terms?

RUPPERT
It means the case has no basis whatsoever in reality – that the judge can see clearly beyond a shadow of a doubt that there is absolutely no evidence to support the claim being made. Or that the attorneys have not come to court sufficiently prepared to present a serious case. Basically that the case is a waste of the taxpayers' money, because the evidence is not there or it's irrelevant. As I said the law is usually used to give a hot shot law firm a slap on the wrist for coming to court without doing their homework or for using the court as a way to delay action against their client. The fines are like warnings.

DJ
Besides this case what was the largest fine ever.

RUPPERT
They said something like $45,000 dollars.

DJ
And were they prepared? Did they do their homework?

RUPPERT
We're almost there. Why don't you ask him yourself?

CUT TO:

INT. – CHRISTIC INSTITUTE OFFICE – DAY

CONVERSATION IN PROGRESS, THE ATTORNEY IS STANDING BEHIND HIS DESK.

ATTORNEY - DANIEL SHEEHAN
We had actual depositions from eye witnesses. We had an office full of lawyers working full time for a year preparing the briefs and the motions. The case was enormous and just preparing it put us close to the edge of bankruptcy, but we knew what we were going up against. Yes, we were more than prepared.

DJ
And they fined you $1.5 million dollars when the largest fine ever was $44,000?

ATTORNEY
(pressing his lips together as if to say it was a long time ago, but it still hurts)
Yup.

DJ
Awww, hell no! We gonna do something about that bullshit. They used some excuse about you not being prepared to bankrupt your firm and shut you up.

CUT TO:

BUSHIDO - OLLIE AND FAWN

EXT. - DUSTY STREET - BEIRUT, LEBANON - DAY

SUBTITLE: "November 3, 1986, Beirut. Lebanon."

Middle Eastern Traditional Music. Seated at small tables outside a bakery, people sip at their coffee as the day breaks. A diesel delivery truck groans as it makes its way past the morning crowd.

CUT TO shot of man on back bumper as he hoists a bundle of newspapers and heaves them at the feet of the PAPER BOY sitting on a wooden box. He looks down and his somewhat bored expression sharpens. He focuses in on the headlines. Close Up of paper in Arabic with Subtitles:

SUBTITLE (FOR NEWSPAPER): “Secret meetings between US and Ayatollah”

SUBTITLE (FOR NEWSPAPER): “United States caught selling missiles to Iran.”

PAPER BOY
(suddenly very awake)
(subtitles): Uncle! Uncle! Look!

UNCLE
(Subtitles) What is it?

PAPER BOY
(in English))
They sold weapons to the Ayatollah!

UNCLE
(English) (shaking head) No... No, can’t be. They are making war on Iran. Let me see.

PAPER BOY
Look! Look!
(hands Uncle a paper)

UNCLE
This is crazy! There will be great problems! Worthless Americans!

Down the street another paper boy has begun shouting out the news:

PAPER BOY 2
EXTRA! EXTRA! US SELLS TOW MISSILES TO AYATOLLAH KHOMEINI!

CUT TO:

INT. - US EMBASSY - LEBANON - DAY

AMBASSADOR
Come on, damn it, pick up! Pick up!
(PHONE RINGING)
(SCREEN SPLITS)

OLIVER NORTH
(asleep at desk, wakes up and picks up)
Yeah, hello, do you have any idea what time it is?

AMBASSADOR
Thank God you're there, I tried your house and nothing, car phone, nothing.

NORTH
OK, OK so you got me, now what is it?

AMBASSADOR
We got a shitstorm!
NORTH
What? What are you talking about?

AMBASSADOR
You gotta clean house, and I mean now! Somebody leaked the fucking weapons sales, and the Lebanese press just put it on the front page! Destroy everything, do you understand me - there's a freaking mob outside this place and they're screaming bloody murder! We gotta disavow, OH FOR FUCKS SAKE

BuShiDo

TELL ME YOU GOT THE SCRAMBLE ON!

NORTH

(starting to panic now) It’s on, its on, FUCK-FUCK-FUCK! Who else knows about this?

M18A1 ‘Claymore’ *antipersonnel mine. Nine inches wide, the mine sprays shrapnel into a “guaranteed casualty area” 50 yards long.* Manufacturer: *Thiokol Corporation (Shreveport, La.); widely imitated.* Cost: *$27.47.* Found in: *Angola, Mozambique, Central America, Southeast Asia.* Number in hiding: *Six million.*

AMBASSADOR
Who doesn't know? Its on the goddam front page! Associated Press called and they'll give me a few hours, but they want a response. What the hell am I gonna tell em, Ollie? What in God's name do I tell them?

NORTH
You don't tell them a GODDAM THING! Do you hear me? "I cannot confirm or deny." That is the only English you know. Cannot confirm or deny. You don't say a fucking word. What is it 0400? What time is it there?

AMBASSADOR
10 AM.

NORTH
OK listen, I will get back to you by - um - um - by 2 pm your time that's 0800 over here. Til then you tell them nothing. Cannot confirm or deny. And you tell 'em if they run anything stateside today - you will guarantee them a full and complete ream job - you got me? Whatever it takes, threats, candy, fucking shoot somebody if you have to - I need 24 hours, goddammit, you got me?!!!!

AMBASSADOR
I'll do what I can, but this thing is out of control. Iraq just called. They want to know what we're doing working both sides of the street? What the hell do I tell them?

NORTH
Cannot confirm or deny. I'll get the lawyers on line, but 'til I get back to you, you don't say a goddam thing, got it?
AMBASSADOR
(hesitant) Oh - kay...

NORTH
Don't OK me! Not now. You gotta contain this thing. Gimme 24 hours. Do it! That is a direct order! I'll call back at 1400 your time. I gotta go. (hangs up.)

North looks frantically around the office. The camera switches to his point of view and zooms in on key items - at same time each change of focus includes a rushing sound:

Whoosh! → FILE CABINET.
Whoosh! → COMPUTER.
Whoosh! → BOXES OF PAPERS

NORTH (CONT'D)
(starts yelling)
Fawn! FAWN!! Get up! GET UP NOW!

(In lower left hand corner of the Screen a time clock appears 04:10:00 AM with the seconds ticking away ' clock stays on screen throughout whole rest of the sequence.)

FAWN HALL
(asleep on a couch in the next room, answers groggily)
What, baby, whaa, what is it?

NORTH
(barking at her)
GET UP NOW!

FAWN HALL
(rolls over and stuffs her head under a pillow)
Not now, sweetie. In the morning baby, I don't feel good.

NORTH
(walks over to sofa bed where Fawn Hall is sleeping)
SOLDIER, GET UP NOW! We got problems. They just blew our cover in Lebanon! We gotta scrub this place clean. NOW GET UP! We are fucked!

FAWN HALL
(bolts upright, hair a mess)
What the hell happened?

NORTH
Lebanese press just put the missile sales on Page Fucking One!

FAWN HALL
(suddenly wide awake, struggles to her feet starts searching for her shoes)
Who the fuck told them?

NORTH
I don't have a goddam idea, but when I do they're getting their clock cleaned. But we got no time to talk - we have to purge these files of every scrap of implicating anything. Please baby, we got maximum 24 hours, maybe a whole lot less.

FAWN HALL
(sputtering)
But .. But... But ....

NORTH
Get dressed. Don't think. Don't think. Just move! I'm going to get files and you've got to go through and find anything and everything that puts us on site in Iran -

FAWN HALL
We need the paper shredder!

NORTH
(nodding yes vigorously to get his own head focussed on the task at hand)
Yes! Good. Probably could use 2, right?

FAWN HALL
(coming to and getting focussed)
There's a real good one in reception. I'll get it. (she heads for the door)

NORTH
(calling after her)
And Fawn?

FAWN HALL
(stopping with the door open)
Yeah?

NORTH
Make some coffee, please, baby.

FAWN HALL
(somewhat annoyed like she is tired of being the maid)
Yes, Colonel.

CUT TO:

MUSIC: "LIFE IN THE FAST LANE" - EAGLES
INT - OLIVER NORTH'S NSC OFFICE - DAWN

It is the same office, but the shot sequence clicks along with very little dialogue, cutting from moment to moment as files are dumped in a growing pile by the 2 small office shredders, that are just not up to the job of handling that amount of paper. The clock in the lower left corner of screen keeps jumping as the pile grows and clear garbage bags are filled with shredded paper. The camera point of view is a bubble lens from the upper corner of the office ceiling (almost as if a security camera was hidden up there and we are seeing the view from that camera)

CUT TO:

(clock says 04:45:00 AM - seconds ticking.)

North is engrossed in trying to unjam the paper shredder

FAWN HALL
What about the shit?

NORTH
The shit?

HALL
The shit!

NORTH
You got shit here?!!!!

HALL
For clients - yes I do... What do we do?

CUT TO:

INT - NSA BATHROOM -DAY

Camera is focussed from inside bathroom on the door, sink, towel dispenser. Fawn Hall bursts through the door. She is tired. She struggles getting the big cardboard box she is carrying into one of the stalls. She finally manages to get the door closed and flicks open a box cutter which she uses to cut the packing tape on a box covered in "Top Secret" and "Eyes Only" stamps. It's crazy - maybe 20 or 30 kilos of cocaine in clear plastic bags - more than a million dollars retail - and she is busy cursing up a storm cutting bags open and flushing them down the toilet.

FAWN HALL
Goddam candy-ass, trust fund babies!!! Little pukes!!!! Fucking Birkenstock sandals and their little faggot communes selling tofu, playing hacky-sack, eating mushrooms all day. Can't do anything!!! Little leeches!!!! Can't make their own money. Couldn't fight their way out of a paper bag! Come and tell us they know how to run the country when all they know how to do is run a bakesale....

Sub-title: "ONE MILLION DOLLARS" in a "cartoon" dialogue box that is bouncing with two arrows pointed at the toilet and at the bags of coke

Fawn Hall looks down at one of the bags she has just cut open - looks over her shoulder for a second and then scoops some coke out the bag with the tip of her boxcutter. She looks over her shoulder again and snorts the coke. A look of relief comes over her face followed by her nose crinkling. She looks around quick for a place to put the bag but it's too late, her face scrunches and she sneezes, blowing coke everywhere, all over the floor and also her face and hair. Close Up of her powder covered face.

FAWN HALL (CONT'D)
Goddammmmmit!!!!!!!!

CUT TO:

INT - OLIVER NORTH'S NSC OFFICE - DAY

NORTH
What the fuck happened?!!!

FAWN HALL
(snarling)
I fucking needed a toot, OK?

NORTH
Baby, there are cameras in the goddam hallways!

FAWN HALL
So?
NORTH
Shit is caked all over your face, for God's sake!

FAWN HALL
What is it all over my face? Oh, shit! Shit! Shit! Shit! Fuck! (Grabs her purse and pulls out a little mirror) Shit! Shit! Shit! Fuuuck! (groans) (starts frantically wiping her face with a napkin) (starts to cry) Goddammit! (screaming) GOD DAMN IT TO HELL!!!!!

NORTH
Baby, don't do this! (grabs her by the shoulders) (pleading) I need you right now, please - just take deep breaths - easy -

easy now. We got to stay on point - just like I taught you.

FAWN HALL
Shut the fuck up! I am so tired with your condescending shit! (mimics) "Baby I need you to stay on point, I need you to make some coffee, I need you to hide these kilos!" Why don't you go get your wife and see if she wants to go to prison instead of me!!!

NORTH
Baby, please calm down -
FAWN HALL
(screaming)
I DON'T HAVE TO FUCKING CALM DOWN!!! IT'S GODDDAMN 5 IN THE MORNING - AND YOU ARE GODDAM LUCKY I'M EVEN STILL HERE.!!!

CUT TO:
INT. US DEA OFFICE - EL SALVADOR DAY

(split screen between El Salvador and Washington/North's office.)

(Clock: 10:17:40 AM - seconds ticking.)

DEA OFFICIAL
Sir, this is DEA - El Salvador.

NORTH
Yes go ahead.

DEA OFFICIAL
Sir, we have a situation. Someone is calling from the press asking if the allegations about Cocaine sales for arms are true.

NORTH
(clamps hand over receiver)
FUCK!... FUCK-FUCK-FUCK-FUCK-FUCK!!!!

DEA OFFICIAL
Sir?

NORTH
Yes! Yes - I mean no. No there is no truth to that.

CUT TO:

DEEP COUNTRY CALLS AGAIN

INT. - RADIO STATION – DAY

DJ
Go ahead next caller you're on the air.

DEEP COUNTRY
Top of the morning to you Mr. Timmons, how are you progressing?

DJ
Is this Mr. Deep Country?

DEEP COUNTRY
Indeed it is. So tell me sir, what has happened since we last spoke? Have you taken time to look into the question I asked you the last time we spoke?

DJ
You mean about Senator Query being involved in the drug smuggling?

DEEP COUNTRY
Not in the smuggling directly – in the confidence scam.

DJ
Oh yeah, now I remember. You said there was a game going on – like 3 card monty.

DEEP COUNTRY
Exactly.

#3
Is that like "Hide the pea?"

DJ
Yeah, yeah, that's like find the red queen, where one of the cards is bent on the corner, and you always think you know right where it is, then he switches it up and takes your money.

#3
And what does this have to do with George Crush selling drugs?

DJ
Yeah, what's all this about?

DEEP COUNTRY
So you haven't looked into this, have you?

DJ
What do you mean I haven't looked into this? Man, this has become my life – this stupid question. I eat it for breakfast, lunch, and dinner.

DEEP COUNTRY
So what have you learned?

DJ
Well, there's a LA Cop who's saying that the government is using Forest Service planes to move tons of cocaine up from El Salvador. Then I just talked to a law firm that brought a suit against the government for selling drugs, and they got hit with the largest fine in the history of the judicial system.

DEEP COUNTRY
What law firm is that?

DJ
The Christic Institute.

DEEP COUNTRY
Oh, of course.

DJ
And then tomorrow I'm supposed to go see a pilot that says he flew the cocaine up from El Salvador. So it isn't exactly like I've been sitting on my ass all day. So if you could help me to help you on this John Query question it would sure speed things up a bit.

DEEP COUNTRY
I know it would, son, but as I said before, it does no good for me to say something, because I cannot testify. You have to develop an airtight case.
AND YOU CAN! I cannot tell you how important it is that you reveal the true nature of these traitors who are pretending to be patriots. The evidence is all there. And there is so much of it! What is needed is someone with the courage and the people skills to put all the pieces of the puzzle together.

DJ
What puzzle is that? What are you talking about?

DEEP COUNTRY
It is not just the Republicans or the Democrats! This is not about just one or the other side of the Senate floor. It is about a totally corrupt set of politicians working in both parties to sell our country to foreign banking interests! And this drug selling is only the tip of the ice berg! We are talking about a second British invasion!

#3
Like the Beatles?

DJ
Man, what are you talking about?

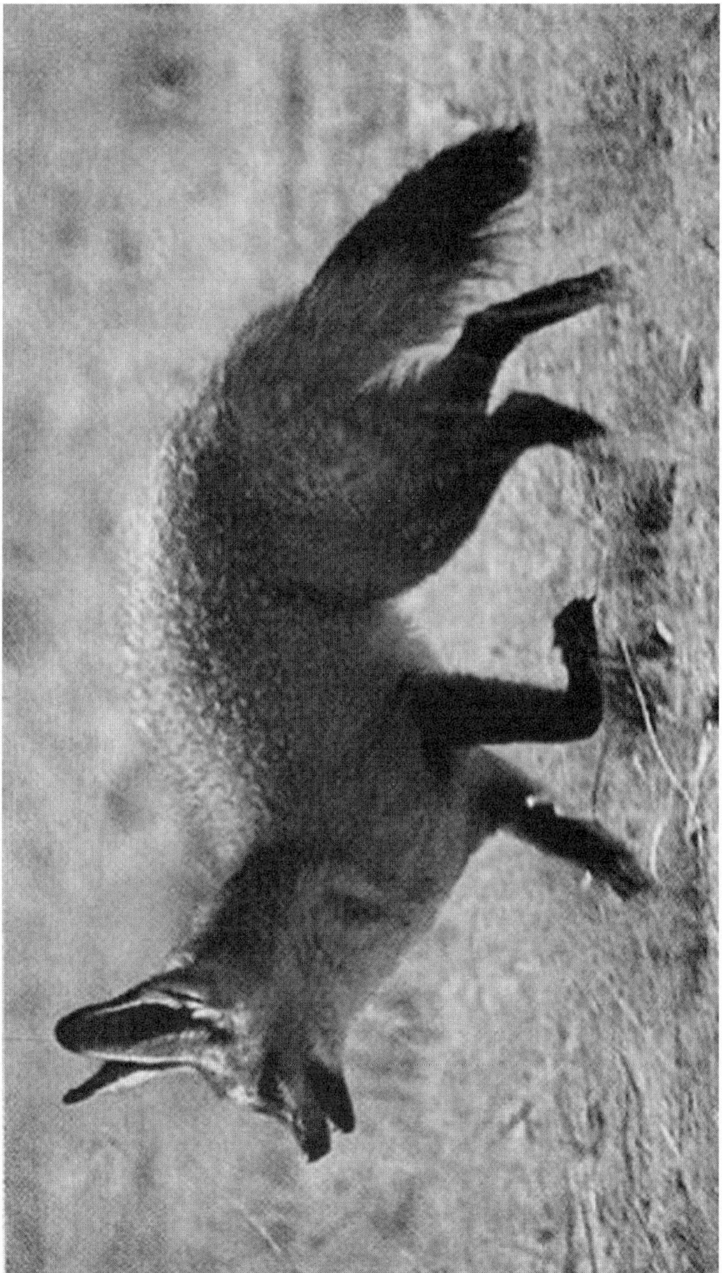

DEEP COUNTRY

I am sorry. I got carried away. My personal beliefs are very deeply held convictions, but I realize that very few people get what I am talking about. Or care for that matter. For right now, let me just say this: It wasn't just the Republicans in this mess. The Democrats were in it up to their eyeballs. And John Query is as deeply involved as any of the Crushes.

DJ

So where do I look? Where do I find the evidence to support this conspiracy of yours?

DEEP COUNTRY

Start with the Christic Institute. They can give you a lot of the background into Query's role in the investigation. And you want to look into their personal history – especially in Viet Nam and also go back and find out where Query and Crush went to college – that is just circumstantial evidence but it is very disturbing nonetheless, considering how hard they tried to convince us that they were on opposite sides of the fence instead of in bed together on this and a wholelot of other nonsense. Look at their college years. And remember what I said about 3 card monty. I have to go now. (click.)

CUT TO:

MUSIC "ILLEGAL BUSINESS" - KRS (REMIX)

THREE CARD MONTY

EXT. - POPPA ZEE'S SHOESHINE STAND – DAY

DJ

So it's like this: I've got most of this thing broken down, and it's starting to scare me.

POPPA ZEE

Then why don't you do the sensible thing and leave well enough alone?

DJ
(resigned)
I don't know.

POPPA ZEE
Boy! What is you doing? You never half step on anything, that's just a ticket to getting your ass whooped. And these here boys they not a joke, do you hear me? Now I told you to leave this thing alone, and you ain't want to listen. You had to go on and gamble your life and a good job and put you and Monica in a heck of a spot, and now you saying you don't know.

DJ
People have been calling the house. Monica's scared. I don't know how they got the number. The kids are scared. This isn't like the other times. I mean people have called the radio station. They've even come to the office and threatened me. But Monica never asked for this.

POPPA ZEE
I told you! Why you got such a thick head about everything?! Look there ain't no way out now but straight through. Once you got on the radio and said what you said and them people called up, it was just like you had stepped in the ring. Now you got to go the distance – the whole 15 rounds – no way back from here, son. Listen you got some money saved up?

DJ
Yeah, a little something.

POPPA ZEE
Look, take this card here, this my nephew, he do security for all the big rap stars when they come through – Puffy Combs and them. You tell him I recommended you, and he'll work with you. He's good at what he does, just tell him everything and make sure you pay that boy on time, mind?

DJ
Yessir.

POPPA ZEE
Now you do that first thing. He over in El Segundo, so straightaway you leave here you get your butt in that fancy car and don't do nothing else 'til that's set. You have any problems you call, you heard?

DJ
Yessir, thank you. (pauses)

POPPA ZEE
Go on, now. You gotta get things secure in your house.

DJ
Yessir. (pause) Poppa Zee?

POPPA ZEE
Yeah?

DJ
There's one more thing that been bugging me all this time.

POPPA ZEE
What is it, child?

DJ
You been listening to the show?

POPPA ZEE
Sometime when I got the time, why?

DJ
There's this man called up call himself Deep Country, say that he got inside information on all this stuff, and he gave me some kind of crazy clue, but for the life of me I can't figure it out.

POPPA ZEE
What he said?

DJ
He said John Query was helping the Crushes to sell the drugs.

POPPA ZEE
You mean Query from the last election, that Query?

DJ
Yessir. He called a few times, and that's all he wants to talk about. An' he said enough other stuff that I think he knows what he's talking about, but I can't figure this one out. He keeps talking about John Query helping Crush to sell, and the only clue he gives is 3 Card Monty.

POPPA ZEE
The card game?

DJ
Yeah.

POPPA ZEE
Well what was Query doing during that big case you was telling me about with the Christian Institute?

DJ
That's the thing, Poppa, Query was the one running the investigation. He was the prosecutor.

POPPA ZEE
And this man what you call - Deep Country – he keep going on about 3 Card Monty?

DJ
Yup.

POPPA ZEE
Maybe Query was working the crowd.

DJ
What you mean working the crowd?

POPPA ZEE
He being the skeptic. Like the dude on the info-mercial who don't believe what the salesman is saying. Hold on, its easier if I show you. Leroy! Boy, come over here for a minute!

LEROY
(runs up)
Yeah?

POPPA ZEE
You got your cards?

LEROY
Yeah.

POPPA ZEE
Play like you was running a game, and I was working the crowd.

LEROY
Wha' for?

POPPA ZEE
(good naturedly playing like he's going to smack Leroy for talking back)
Boy! Don't you ever ask me what – just make the cards work! Like I got time to 'splain every damn thing!
(Leroy sets up on a nearby picnic table and starts shuffling the cards, calling out to an imaginary crowd)

LEROY
Where she at? Find the red lady and get paid daily! Where she at? There she is. Place your bets. Lay that money down right here, honey! I must be crazy giving my money away each and every day! Place your bets!

POPPA ZEE
(walking up like he just came down the street)
Boy what is this nonsense here! You got your cards all bent up, don't know what you doing. She right there plain as day.

LEROY
Where she at? Where she at, old man? Right here, there she go. Whoop, where she go? Where she at?

POPPA ZEE
Right there you damn fool, center card.

LEROY
Put your money where your mouth is, old man, or you ain't saying nothing.

POPPA ZEE
She right there.

LEROY
So put your money down!

POPPA ZEE
I don't gamble. But with your slow ass hands, you shouldn't neither. She right there!

LEROY
Where? Which one?

POPPA ZEE
On the left.

LEROY
On the left?

POPPA ZEE
Are you deaf? Yeah, on the left.

LEROY
Is he right? Does he know? Here we go! Man you were right you coulda walked off with twenty just like that. Too slow for your own good! Place your bets right to left! This is what's next! Place your bets!

POPPA ZEE
She right there. Man, you are one sorry ass playa. I should take your money just to show you how you shoulda stayed in school.

LEROY
Go ahead, old man, take my money, you know, might do me some good. You sure your cataract eyes is seeing the table right? How many fingers on my hand old man? Where does the lady stand? Find the statue of liberty and double your money.

POPPA ZEE
Cataracts my ass, a blind man with a seeing eye dog could take your money! She right there.

LEROY
Right there? Whoop, there it is, that's another $20 you coulda had, except you ain't got no money.

POPPA ZEE
I ain't got no money! Here sucker, pay me (drops a $20 on the table) She right there!

LEROY
Where?

POPPA ZEE
There!

LEROY
Lookie Lookie let's see what's cookie. Hey, there you go old man, there's your $20. What you say we double it up?

POPPA ZEE
(picks up the $20, steps out of character)
OK, now Cassius, you see what just happened, right? I come up and pretend to be just part of the crowd, and I get the crowd going. That's working the crowd. You part of the scam but you playing a role – the skeptic – the guy who don't believe. When

the con man convinces the guy working the crowd, then other people decide to buy in. Now there's different ways to work the crowd. At an auction the guy working the crowd drives the price up. On TV, it's the guy who doesn't believe that you can actually cook a burger on your car's engine. When you convince him, the crowd believes -

DJ
(continuing his thought)
- because he asked all the right questions.

POPPA ZEE
Precisely.

DJ
So Query played the prosecutor when the lawsuit came down and asked only the safe questions, and then he believed all the answers Crush gave him.

POPPA ZEE
Maybe.

DJ
It has to be. Because there was a lot more evidence that Query left alone, all that stuff the Christic Institute threw at Crush and got swept under the rug. But they had to have some kind of official investigation so Query ran that shit to keep from going too deep. Did you know they went to school together?

POPPA ZEE
Who?

DJ
Crush and Query. They were in the same fraternity, some crazy frat called Cults and Thrones.

POPPA ZEE
What it called?!

DJ
Cults and Thrones.

POPPA ZEE
Now that is some fucked up shit!

LEROY
Hey man, what about my $20 dollars!

POPPA ZEE
Leroy you been owing me $40 since last month!

LEROY
I know that, and I get paid on Friday, and I'll get it to you then...

POPPA ZEE
That's what you said the last 3 Fridays running.

DJ
Look I gotta go deal with this security thing. Thanks for everything.

POPPA ZEE
Call me soon as you got it set up just so's I don't worry.

DJ
Bet.

LEROY
(scene fades out as he's saying)
Naw, man, I need that money for my baby's formula...

CUT TO:

EXT - TIMMONS' HOUSE - NIGHT

A Security Guard in casual clothes is sitting in his car accross the street from the Timmons' driveway. He has his hands in his Starter jacket. His cell phone chirps.

VOICE
What's crackin'?

SECURITY GUARD
Everything's cool.

INT - TIMMONS' LIVING ROOM - NIGHT

The DJ's wife throws her hands up in desperation. There are beads of sweat on her forehead, and they got Central A/C...

MONICA TIMMONS
Baby, just explain to me what are you getting us into? And don't you try and rationalize or talk down to me. Who the hell are those people in front of the house. Scared the shit out of my brother. Is this your latest crusade to save the children?

DJ
They're security, baby. I don't like it, but -

MONICA
But nothing! Those aren't security, those are hoodlums in uniforms!

DJ
They're not hoodlums - (explaining) Poppa knows them.

MONICA
Zee?!!! You went to your block, and you couldn't come to me? - Cassius!

DJ
It's a precaution - just in case -

MONICA
In case what?! In case the FBI comes knocking on the front door?! How is a bunch of Zee's hoodlum nephews gonna make

the Government back off. They just gonna make 'em more suspicious!

DJ
It's not for the government...

MONICA
Who's it for, then, huh, Mr. Ask a Damn Stupid Question everybody already know the answer to? (almost screaming) WHO'S IT FOR, DAMMIT?! THAT'S MY DAMN QUESTION; WHO'S IT FOR, CASSIUS?! THE NRA?! THE KKK?! THE DAMN CIA?! CASSIUS, WHAT ARE YOU DRAGGING THIS FAMILY INTO?!!!

CUT:

EXT. – TIMMONS' HOUSE - NIGHT

SECURITY GUARD
(panick in his voice)
Cassius, Get Up!!!

CUT TO:

INT – TIMMONS' HOUSE – BEDROOM

Cassius and Monica Timmons are asleep in their bed. The Security Guard's yelling wakes him up.

DJ
Huh, wha'?

SECURITY GUARD
(off screen)
Cassius, GET UP!!!!

DJ
I'm up I'm up, what the, what's going on?

SECURITY GUARD
Cassius NOW!

Cassius looks out the window. One of the Security Guards is standing on top of his car, and as he stares out the window in shock he sees a virtual stampede of animals: Dogs, cats, rats, snakes, possums, rabbits, coyotes, deer – a herd of deer – jumping fences and cars setting off alarms and breaking windshields in a panicked full tilt sprint – where? – East. Away from the Ocean.

INDONESIA. The animals knew. TIDAL WAVE!!!

SECURITY GUARD
(looking up at the DJ, his jaw trembling)
What is this? How - wha? I-ya -

DJ
Monica!!! GET THE KIDS, BABY, NOW!!!!

He rips back the screen to the window and jumps onto the porch roof, looking down at this kid called himself CUJO coming apart at the seams, the security guard looking back at him, and then he heard it – a *rushing* sound – him and Cujo freeze looking through the trees back where the animals were still running form – WHERE? – DAMMIT!!! WHERE WAS IT?!!! CAN'T SEE SHIT!!!!. And then he saw it – in the sky. It was like a cloud of flies, locusts some shit – a mile wide dropping from heaven like a black rain – the rushing sound coming in fast:

PHHITTT!!! THIT-DIT-DDITT!!!
PHIT – THIBBIDIT – DIT – DIDDIDDITTT – THRRRIPPP – BIT – DIBBIBITTT!!!!

Sweeping over the neighbor's lawn like an advancing wall of rain, pinging on the asphalt, fracturing windshields and then bursting tires, cutting leaves in the trees to shreds, sticking in fence posts, tree trunks → long stainless steel needles yellowed with some kind of resin – Cujo was screaming holding his arms over his head and then collapsed on the roof of the car

– writhing in pain

PHHITTT!!! THIT-DIT-DDITT!!!
PHIT – THIBBIDIT – DIT – DIDDIDDITTT – THRRRIPPP
– BIT – DIBBIBITTT!!!! THIBBIBBIT!!! THRIDIPIDIDIT!!!

Cassius dove for the window, needles hitting like swarming bees, stinging and then numbing – his muscles were slowing and his mind was distant →"What is happening?" → "Who cares?" He was falling down, down, hitting the downy – the downy? – no matter – he was there – the ground was there. He fell through a 100 down quilts – quilted by slaves – How? – The Ground had him now – He was going home – "Can't run no more, Cassius" – Cassie? – Can't run no more.... Where you at, Cassie?

CUT TO:

It was like he was in a fish tank, the water was warm –
And salty.
Was it a mortuary? an underwater insane asylum? Something was swimming in his brain – a lost thought – so close – "tiny purple fishes run laughing through your fingers" – Eric Clapton? – Cream – "Cash Rules Everything Around Me – CREAM!!!! Get the Money – Dollar Dollar Bill, y'all...."

Where you at, Cassie?

It's warm. Warm and wet on my head – oozing sticky warm

Why the table broken?

Who broke – ?

Monica Timmons screamed.

That woke him up. He was lying in broken glass – the dining room table – how did I get downstairs?

MONICA TIMMONS

BuShiDo

(stress almost choking her voice)
I need an ambulance at –

The kids were screaming - they were so scared...

EXT. – EAST LOS ANGELES – THE DJ'S OLD NEIGHBORHOOD – DAY

Cassius walks down a secluded block. There's a set of girls playing double dutch across the street

DOUBLE DUTCH GIRLS
Miss Mary Mack! Mack! Mack!
All dressed in black! black! black!
With silver buttons! Buttons! Buttons!
Up and down her back! back! back!
I saw your friends! friends! friends!
Coming down the track! track! track!
Ain't got no ends! ends! ends!
Cause they momma's on crack! crack! crack!

Cassius walks down another few houses and rings the doorbell. This is his Grandmother's house, where he comes every Thanksgiving and Christmas even if it's only to have some leftovers and dessert. His grandmother somes bustling up to the screen door to see who it is.

GRANDMA
(bursting into a big smile, her eyes brimming with tears)
Oh my heavens, it's you!!!

DJ
Hi Grandma.

GRANDMA
What in Jesus name happened to your head?

DJ
I'm not sure, Gramma

GRANDMA
(looking him up and down and knitting her forehead into a wrinkled mass of concern)
Baby.... Come on in the house, lemme take a look at you! We got work to do.

DJ
Gramma, I - I had this dream.

GRANDMA
Yes, child, I felt something yesterday – didn't know what it was – now I can see –

DJ
See what, Gramma? –

GRANDMA
You hush, everything is fine, it's just good you came.

DJ
What is it?

GRANDMA
It's nothing, baby, nothing at all, but we going to see a friend of mine over to the church.

DJ
Gramma don't get upset.

GRANDMA
God Damned Devil!!!

DJ
Gramma, how you cursing?

GRANDMA
Ain't nothing wrong with cursing a devil!
Same thing as praising the Lord!
I'd rather be praising the Lord, but sometimes you gotta show

a devil who the True Lord and Master *is*.

It's when what you say got no belief in it – that's the worst problem they is. You going to church every Sunday, saying Jesus have mercy this and God show me the light, and God come down from heaven and be with me in this darkest hour and Heal Me Jesus! – but you ain't believing God *can* still do those things. You feeling so lost that you think well maybe Miracles used to happen, but they can't still happen today... You not believing any more!

That is the worst thing that can happen to you, son. That is what they mean by someone taking the Lord's name in vain. Either you done lost hope, or you don't want God to see what you doing cause you doing wrong and you hoping to get away with it.

Never say, Jesus Help Me – if you don't believe God can help you. You should never ever say God when you don't mean it with your heart. Say "Help me so I can see you again God – restore my sight."

(she knocks her head with her knuckles for emphasis)

In my book, taking God's name in vain take all the power out your belief. Put your money where your mouth is. If you don't know what you saying then keep quiet. It's that simple.

If I see someone who sick and looking to get healed, I'ma do my best to heal them like Jesus said – freely give as you have freely received. But if I see someone sick – with a devil all up in 'em, twisting they insides and making them crazy and they come around my babies trying to get them into the same poison and lose they minds, then, baby seeing is believing – I see a devil – and can't no one tell me I ain't – and just like I praise God, well same way I'ma curse a devil. It might not be perfect – Lord know I got a ways to go to understand why God even made devils– but I got too strong a love for my own not to curse a devil coming round here like some dog with rabes looking to kill my flesh and blood!

Now go on and wash up and change your clothes, we gon' go out to Pastor's country house before it get too dark – and leave all your things here, 'specially that damn cell phone!

CUT TO:

John Kerry takes a dive.

INT. DEMOCRATIC NATIONAL ELECTION HEADQUARTERS - 10 AM

SUB-TITLE: "Democratic HQ Day After 2004 Election"

It is the day after the 2004 Presidential Elections, and a large crowd is milling around, talking and yelling. There are people shouting up at the podium, where John Query is standing getting ready to address the crowd:

CROWD 1
What about Cincinatti?

CROWD 2
10 hours in a goddamn line waiting to vote? What are you gonna do?!!!!

ETC

JOHN QUERY
(steps to podium, taps mic, and clears throat)

People applaud loudly, cheering.

WHOLE CROWD
(chanting)
Query! Query! Query!

QUERY
(motioning for crowd to settle down)
Ladies and gentlemen, please, please....
Quiet down, please, PLEASE! ....please.
(crowd quiets down)
Thank you.

BuShiDo
I know you've been wondering about the - um - "Ir - regularities" in last night's election.

CROWD
You damn straight!!!

More shouts.

QUERY
(continuing over noise)
There were people standing out in the cold waiting for hours who never got a chance to vote. Many others who doubtless turned away before the polls closed.
(pause)
I was told that the exit polls in many states we lost predicted victory for our side. Very unusual. Some would say statistically impossible even.
We are hearing a lot - I mean a lot - of rumors and even verified reports of electoral fraud - that is to say fixed elections, ballot boxes being lost or even stolen, electronic voting machines that were tampered with. Recounts that have been made impossible because there are no paper records to recount - only electronic data that has been collected without the ability to check it's authenticity, and so on....
As you would imagine, myself and Mrs. Heinz-Ketchup-Kerry have too many lawyers on retainer ready and waiting to do whatever is necessary to ensure that our democratic process stays democratic - and to fully investigate any illegal stacking of the deck -

CROWD 4
That's right!

QUERY
- that may have occurred.
In this great country, every vote should count!!! (wild applause starts). Because in this great country, we are not going back to the days of poll taxes! (stabs finger in air) - Jim Crow laws! (stabs finger) -

CROWD 4
That's right!

QUERY
- or any of these low-down, dirty tactics that are used to deny citizens the right to vote! (finger)

CROWD 4
That's right! You tell 'em!!!

(applause gets louder and louder - a freaking standing ovation)

QUERY
(makes motion to crowd to quiet down and they gradually do)
So, it will probably come as a bit of a shock to many of you that I am throwing in the towel, as they say.

(crowd gasps)

I know it's only 10 AM, and most of the recounts haven't even really begun, and I really do want to apologize for this - but I am just exhausted. This campaign just seemed to go on forever and a day.

(dead silence)

Matter of fact, if this thing drags on another hour, I don't think I could stand it. I'm tired, my wife's tired, the family's just begging me for some kind of a vacation, and in about half an hour as a matter of fact, we have a plane to catch.
Now, I do want to thank all of you for the millions of hours you have put in volunteering, working the polls, collecting signatures, driving people to the polls - all of that important and vital activity that makes our country such a great democracy.
Especially the high school dropouts working at McDonalds or in the National Guard.
I want to assure you that none of your effort was in vain.
We gave them a solid run for their money.

We made them sweat.
We even made them resort to unfair tactics.
That - in and of itself is a kind of victory.
Really.
Any time you give your all - when you give 110%, and you go to the wall trying to make something happen - then nobody can really call you a loser. Not in my book. Not in Jack Kennedy's book, either, I would bet! You here standing in this hall today - you are all winners.
I know this.
God knows this.
The whole world knows this!

(pause)

CUT TO:

INT. - LIVING ROOM IN NICARAGUA - DAY
(same living room with FAT OLD MEN AND WOMEN from when Hasenfus was shot down, drinking beer watching speech on TV.)

FAT MAN
Que mierda dijo?
(subtitle: What shit did he say?)

FAT WOMAN
(looking over shoulder)
Que todos son ganadores.
(sub-title: That we're all winners.)

CUT BACK TO QUERY:

QUERY
But at this early hour I have to admit that what we as a country need is unity.
(spells it out)
U-N-I-T-Y.
That is what we need. The country has spoken. We have been

given a message.
Even if that message is somewhat scrambled and a bit unclear and maybe yes maybe even a complete forgery - We still have been given a message.
And that message is what matters now.
Not a few votes burning in a trash can in some Cincinatti alleyway - No!
Not some crazy exit pollsters raking muck about highly unusual discrepancies! No!
Not some crazy debate about discarded absentee ballots or punches that weren't punched or maybe they were - none of that!

(Close up of Mrs. Ketchup-Query rolling her eyes at that last sentence like "What an asshole!")

QUERY (CONT)
No! No! NO! That is not what we need.
We need rest. (pause)
Relaxation. (pause)
(lowers voice in fatherly tone)
Time to heal.
That's what we need.
And as long as I'm here - in this most important time and place - that is what we are going to get...
Thank you, God bless you,
!AND SEE YOU IN 2008!!!!
(waves hand to crowd and goes to hug family)

CUT TO:

(sea of faces - jaws dropped - it is so quiet you can hear a pin drop)

(sound of crickets chirping)

CUT TO :

CAMPAIGN MANAGER and TV NEWS PRODUCER in TV

Booth looking at eachother like "DO SOMETHING!"

CAMPAIGN MANAGER
He's fucking dying out there!!!

TV NEWS PRODUCER
Cue applause now!!!
And get that band up off their ass and make some music!!!
DO IT!!!!

CUT TO:

(Close up of "APPLAUSE" sign flashing like an air raid siren, as you hear a marching band diving into some John Phillips Sousa 4th of July Fireworks music.)

CUT TO

Confetti and balloons falling from the ceiling.

Out of nowhere people begin applauding and cheering, CUT TO Query with Family on stage waving to crowd as applause grows louder and people cheer more and more.

CUT.

MUSIC: 2ND ROUND KNOCKOUT - Canibus and Wyclef
"I'm sorry. If you need assistance please check the number and dial again."

CUT TO:

INT - RADIO STATION DJ BOOTH - DAY

(conversation in progress. Music is playing on air:..)
MUSIC "WHERE WERE YOU WHILE WE WERE GETTING HIGH?" – OASIS

....and the DJ is trying desperately to get Ruppert to listen to him before they have to get back on the air)

DJ
So it's just another mafia?

RUPPERT
No, you're missing the main point!!!

DJ
Damn it, well what is the *main* point?

RUPPERT
The main point is that in another few years, we are all going to run out of oil, and every government in the world is getting ready to deal with that. What I am doing is laying out a more accurate map of the world. Because you can't get anywhere in this world if you don't know what the world looks like.

DJ
(a bit annoyed by the long winded constantly meandering "map" business)
So what? You know you sound less like a cop and more like an intellectual wannabee professor of military history who got cut loose from Annapolis for mental health reasons. I don't have time to go back and figure out what Ghengis Khan or the Taliban has to do with oil money, when all I want to know is did the damn Government sell drugs or not. You - You like a Jehovah's Witness - I can't get you to focus!

RUPPERT
It isn't a sound byte! If you want to understand the events leading up to 9/11 and the meaning of the war in Afghanistan -

DJ
That's just it! I didn't ask you for the answer to every question in the world about current events. I don't know how to make this any clearer! Not everybody thinks like you do! Let me put it another way: VERY FEW people read books all day. Even if they had the time - most people don't want to!

BuShiDo

Face Facts! You have a very rare opportunity to wake people up - but instead you seem cursed by your wacky ass up-bringing to put people to sleep! Now take it for what it's worth, but in my opinion - with you and what you say to people --> LESS IS MORE! Capiche?

RUPPERT

You don't understand. I am like the expert witness at a trial on war crimes. We have to start a movement!

DJ

Brother, I understand more about moving people up out of their seat - in a church, at a picnic, even at a boring ass stuffy University auditorium - than you with your Encyclopedic knowledge of minute details will EVER know.

RUPPERT

But -

The SOUND ENGINEER buzzes in on the intercom:

SOUND ENGINEER

You're back live in 5, Cassius

DJ

(to Engineer)

Hold on, Curtis! - just play another song - we ain't ready yet.

Curtis puts on "MY PHILOSOPHY" - KRS-1

DJ (CONT'D)

(to Ruppert)

But nothing. You want to be the expert witness? Perfect. I can work with that. Now, since I met you - what was it last week? - you have given me 3 big ass college level books with more footnotes than actual writing. Is that correct, Mr. Expert Witness?

RUPPERT

I -

DJ
Ah, Ah, Ah - just answer the damn question, please.

RUPPERT
Yes I did.

DJ
And - Mr. Expert Witness - did you on that same occasion only one week ago - did you give me 2 long, boring ass CD's with you lecturing up and down World History, Advanced Micro and Macro Economic Theory and Practice, along with what sounded to me like an introduction to the Political Geography of the Middle East, Columbia, and Central Asia including a bunch of countries ending in "-stan" that so help me God I never ever heard of - Did you do that?

RUPPERT
I cannot explain the nature -

DJ
Kwame, direct the "expert witness" to answer the damn question, please.

KWAME
He is arrogant, but there is a useful purpose here.

RUPPERT
(exhaling to get past his frustration)
Yes. - OK? Yes, I am long winded.

DJ
Let the court records show that the expert witness is referring to himself as "long winded."

KWAME
So noted.

DJ

Mr. Expert Witness, when exactly did you expect me to find the time in my very busy schedule to review all this voluminous excess of information over-load?

RUPPERT

(shoulders slumping)

I don't know.

DJ

(to Kwame with an exhale of satisfaction)

He does not know. That, I believe, is a first in our short history together. Mr. Ruppert, do you realize that I stayed up until 1 AM for several nights in a row - denying my wife her right to a foot massage among various other things - all in order that I might extract what you so ludicrously refer to as "sound-bytes" from your long-ass, never ending digressions into Who's Who in the CIA, the New York Stock Exchange, and Corporate America?

RUPPERT

(playing along)

I was not aware.

DJ

I did indeed. And I am not ashamed to tell the court that I am somewhat pleased with myself for having done so. I can honestly tell you that I did not feel as if I had wasted my time. Now. Answer the following questions and please be direct: Are you a former Los Angeles Narcotics Detective?

RUPPERT

I am.

DJ

Do you believe that the government of the United States sold large quantities of drugs to it's own citizens starting in the late 50's and continuing on through the mid 80's - said drugs to have included heroin and cocaine in excess of several hundred tons net weight?

RUPPERT
Yes sir I do.

DJ
Why do you believe that? Did you yourself witness government officials employed by the CIA transporting quantities of cocaine on a scale that would support such a statement? In other words, are you - a former LAPD Narcotics Detective - telling me that you saw such cocaine shipments with your own eyes?

RUPPERT
Yes sir, I did.

DJ
And are you also telling me that you believe the US Govt and its agents are responsible for the majority of the increase in cocaine imports during the period 1980 to 1988?

RUPPERT
Yes, I believe that would be a correct assessment.

DJ
Can you tell the court how much of a change was there in cocaine importation during the period 1980 to 1988?

RUPPERT
By my estimates - there was about 70 to 80 metric tons per year coming in during 1980, and that increased to approximately 600 metric tons per year coming in by 1988.

DJ
So that would be an increase of about 520 tons every year for 8 years making a grand total of over 40,000 EXTRA tons - not pounds or kilos - tons. Is my math correct on that score?

RUPPERT
(pauses)
It is.

DJ
You know that you are under oath?

RUPPERT
Yes sir, I do know.

DJ
Do you wish to change any of those statements in the light of the fact that you may be perjuring yourself in front of your peers and God?

RUPPERT
No sir, I do not.

DJ
No further questions.

Volume goes up on MUSIC: "MY PHILOSOPHY" KRS - ONE →"...rhyming for the King, am I wrong? (echo...)"

CUT TO:

SALVADOR'S DREAM

SALVADOR AND CRUSH DUST IT UP

INT. LOCKER ROOM OF NATIONALS STADIUM - DAY

FAR AWAY SHOT OF SALVADOR AND HIS MANAGER FROM ACROSS THE ROOM. SALVADOR IS WAVING HIS HANDS LIKE "NO WAY!"

MOVE TO 2 SHOT SALVADOR AND MANAGER.

MANAGER
Salvador, what is the problem here?

SALVADOR
I just don' want to go, OK? Please make son' excuses, tell them

I am busy or I have a cold or anything like that. OK?

MANAGER
He's the President of the United States for God's Sake!! You don't lie or make excuses. This is a great honor, for crying out loud. You know how many people would kill to be in your shoes?

SALVADOR
(looking manager straight in the eye)
I - Don't - Want - To - Be - There. Please.

MANAGER
(puts on his no bullshit face)
Salvador, you will be out there, and you will greet the President. The owner told me, and I am telling you. I don't have time for this right now. Do you understand - the President is here and I got a million other problems way bigger than your cold feet or whatever the hell this is. Don't be nervous. He puts his pants on one leg at a time just like you and me.

SALVADOR
I am no nervous...

MANAGER
(losing patience)
Whatever it is, Salvador, I just don't have time -

SALVADOR
Then -

MANAGER
Salvador, I got NO time for this - Suit up and get out there, NOW!

SALVADOR
Yessir.....

CUT TO:

EXT - WASHINGTON NATIONALS BASEBALL STADIUM - DAY

AERIAL SHOT OF THE STADIUM, FILLED TO CAPACITY, AND CROWD NOISES.

CUT TO:

SHOT OF PITCHER'S MOUND, PRESIDENT CRUSH ON THE MOUND, TALKING WITH THE MANAGER.

ANNOUNCER #1

The Washington Nationals - a team already plagued by pitching problems - find themselves suddenly a young team looking to rebuild with a new manager. And with us today to throw out the first pitch, President George Crush, a former owner of a baseball club - the Texas Rangers - talking with the owner of the Nationals, getting ready to start off the season for Washington. The President finishing up his conversation, steps to the mound, winds up, and here's the pitch. Not a bad arm. Looked like a strike. Was that a fast ball or a slider, you think?

ANNOUNCER #2

Looked more like a change up from here. We don't have the radar gun set up, but still looks like he has a pretty good arm.

ANNOUNCER #1

And now he's going over to say hello to the coaching staff coming out to greet him... There's Laura Crush waving to the crowd....

And there seems to be some kind of a hold up now - the President taking some time to talk to 3rd base coach Salvador Fuentes, seeming somewhat hesitant -

ANNOUNCER #2

He seems more than just hesitant, he seems like he doesn't - wait a minute -

ANNOUNCER 1

Did he just spit?

ANNOUNCER #2
And the President does not like that one bit. This is getting a little out of hand...

ANNOUNCER 1
A somewhat heated exchange going on - somebody better get in there - the President not at all pleased with Coach Fuentes' attitude - HOLY SHIT!

ANNOUNCER #2
AND HE'S DOWN! HE JUST KNOCKED HIM DOWN! DID YOU SEE THAT?!!! SECURITY IS RUSHING THE FIELD!!! -

ANNOUNCER 1
What the - ? All hell has broken loose on the field! The President is down! Both benches up on the field - Secret Service agents - I CAN'T BELIEVE IT! THIS IS CHAOS!!!

ANNOUNCER #2
THEY JUST CLUBBED SOMEBODY! THIS IS A RIOT, FOR GOD'S SAKE!

CUT TO:

INT - STUDIO - SPORTS SHOW - DAY

ANNOUNCER #1
Now what do you make of?

ANNOUNCER #2
What were the stats on this?

ANNOUNCER #1
Well we got quite a few people in the hospital. I mean, can you do that?

ANNOUNCER #2
Obviously, he did..

ANNOUNCER #1
Well, yeah, but what is the penalty for something like that? I mean you're not talking a ten game suspension here.

ANNOUNCER #2
This has got to be handled by the legal system.

ANNOUNCER #1
But what's the charge? Bodyslamming the Commander in Chief?
How did this happen? I mean he knew. He had to know. You don't come from Mexico -

ANNOUNCER #2
- El Salvador

ANNOUNCER #1
- I'm sorry El Salvador - and not know that this means the end of your career - and maybe even deportation. So why throw away your career - not to mention your citizenship - I just don't get it -

CUT TO:

MOTHER AND SISTER
(scared and crying on Local TV:)
Where is he?!!!!

CUT TO:

REPORTER
...and actually at this moment we are not exactly sure where they are detaining Salvador Fuentes, although police have assured us that he is safely in custody at an undisclosed location.

CUT BACK TO FAMILY:

BROTHER
(pushing forward to speak)
Listen, we know that what Salvador did is wrong. He is a very good person, and this is not like him at all. We know he have done wrong. We only wish to explain that he lose his wife and

children to American bombing in El Salvador, and so he stay angry from this, because he love them very much.

CUT TO:

SALVADOR'S MANAGER
(press conference mikes pressed close to his sweating face)
He asked me repeatedly if he could be excused from the ceremony. He asked me not to go. He is not to my knowledge a man given to violence, and I have known him for many years. Apparently there was a situation back in El Salvador - where he was born -

CUT TO:

LEAGUE PRESIDENT
.....the stiffest penalty possible (CUT) the league wants to make it clear that it does not and will NEVER tolerate behavior of this kind -

CUT TO:

TEAMMATE
All I know is he's a good man.

REPORTERS
(shouting questions)

TEAMMATE
I - I - I don't know about all that - He's a good man - that's what I can tell you.

CUT TO:

CRUSH
We - Laura and I - bear no ill will to Coach Fuentays or towards the peoples of El Salvador -

CUT TO:

TV COMMERCIAL - MEN OF THE SQUARE TABLE - IN PROGRESS

The Men of the Square Table sit in session, bottled beer all around, with the old man in the corner waiting - pen poised - to record the deliberations on the important issues of today.

SINBAD
Body slamming the Commander in Chief!!! (winces in fake pain) - What is the ruling on that?

EDDIE GRIFFIN
Was it a full body slam?

GOV. JESSE "THE BODY" VENTURA
(clarifying the point)
Double leg take down.

MACHO CAMACHO (BOXER)
Why they stop the fight? He bleeding?

TIM ALLEN (HOME IMPROVEMENT)
The point is (hands waving in the air to find the phrase) - you can't do that!

AL (FROM HOME IMPROVEMENT)
Exactly!!!

CHUCK NORRIS
What if we went around, attacking other presidents, or putting funny stuff in Fidel Castro's cigars?

MACHO CAMACHO (MEXICAN BOXER)
So what?!!! It come with the job! He no shoot hin. He jus' push hin aroun' a leetle. No even too mush. You can't torture hin' for like doin' like that (makes pushing motion with his hands) Is no like Crush make of glass. He no going break in half! Put Salvador in prison, j'OK - Up State, j'OK - but no Guantanamo with no sleep and crazy military police. NO! I don' allow!!!

AL (FROM HOME IMPROVEMENT)
Is Salvador even a US citizen?

MACHO CAMACHO
How can he play baseball for 20 years, and be a coach, an' all a that, and no be a citizen?

YAO (FROM THE NBA)
(only man at the table with a Sake bottle in front of him)
He must to be full citizen for that if he complete so long time in country.

TIM ALLEN
Yeah, but how many generations are we talking here?

MACHO CAMACHO
How many generation? How about 400 generation before Colombo coming to Mexico stinking of bad breath?

AL (FROM HOME IMPROVEMENT)
Peter Falk?

EDDIE GRIFFIN
(sounding drunk)
He's a citizen!!! I say 30 days and a order of protection!

CHUCK NORRIS
An order of protection?!!!

EDDIE GRIFFIN
An order of protection: Salvador can' t come within 500 feet of the President.

CHUCK NORRIS
You mean a thousand yards!

EDDIE GRIFFIN
A thousand yards?!!! You tryin' ta make this some kind a "Day of the Jackal" Terrorist Incident. This ain't the Last Boyscout!

- He wasn't creeping around in a flak jacket! - (jabbing in the air with his hand for emphasis) He spit on the ground to let the man know what was up!!! Crush caught a attitude, and he popped him. One time. Didn't even punch the man once! Where's the beef?

CHUCK NORRIS (sarcastic)
All right you tell me what this is then.

EDDIE GRIFFIN
To me it looks like Domestic Violence... (grinning)

CHUCK NORRIS
You're not funny and I'm not buying. Burt?

BURT REYNOLDS
(rubbing his chin, looking straight at Chuck Norris)
Looks like a bar fight to me.

MACHO CAMACHO
E' sactly!!!

CHUCK NORRIS
He was in the Salvadoran military for Christ's Sake!

GOV. JESSE "THE BODY" VENTURA
Yeah, but he was fighting on our side. I've seen this before.

MACHO CAMACHO
Yeah, he was working for you government!

EDDIE GRIFFIN
30 days and mandatory AA Meetings for a year, maybe some of that PTSD massage therabee they got over at the VA...

CHUCK NORRIS
(staring at Eddie Griffin like he might smack him)
How much do you weigh?

EDDIE GRIFFIN
It's not how much I weigh, Grasshopper, it's how much my manager weighs (puts on "Tony Montana" accent) j'OK, my frien'?

GOV. JESSE "THE BODY" VENTURA
(speaking to Burt Reynolds)
I can't accept that.

BURT REYNOLDS
(back to Jesse)
What do you think?

GOV. JESSE "THE BODY" VENTURA
3 years - minimum security - but 3 years. He lost his head. Every soldier knows rule #1. He's retired, but - officially - you can't condone striking an officer - no matter how stupid -

AL (FROM HOME IMPROVEMENT)
Exactly!!!

CHUCK NORRIS
(like a counter offer)
5 years. 3 with good behavior.

BURT REYNOLDS
But no Guantanamo?

EDDIE GRIFFIN
Hells no!!!!

MACHO CAMACHO
E' sactly!!!!

GOV. JESSE "THE BODY" VENTURA
Man Law?

EVERYBODY
Man Law.

CUT TO:

INT. – GUANTANAMO BAY PRISON – DAY

(for Spanish to English translation see pages 218-227)

MUSIC: (Ranchera (Mexican) ("Es un Caballo muy bueno" – Silvio Rodriguez)

Subtitle: "Maximum Security Terrorist Containment Facility - Guantanamo Bay, Cuba"

We see Salvador as he is finger-printed, searched, given prison clothes, etc in rapid succession. He walks into his high security cell (solitary) and goes to sleep. He wakes up the next morning,

CUT TO:

Salvador walking down the hall for breakfast . Suddenly a bomb explodes and knocks the guards down, and a group of STAR WARS EWOKS (that's right) with bands of ammo slung across their teddy bear chests come running up. Surprisingly, the little brown Ewoks speak Spanish:

EWOK #1
Vamanos, Buey! No tenemos mucho tiempo!

They run down the hall, dodging occasional bullets, and jump on their Ewok air scooters, firing away, waiting for Salvador to jump on. Whooosh! They take off shooting bursts at the guard towers who are shooting at them.

Helicopters swing in behind them as they fly over and away over the Cuban Highlands. They fly through trees and canyons, with the helicopters firing away.

In one helicopter, a BAD NAZI GRINGO is cursing at the PILOT.

BAD NAZI GRINGO
How can you keep misszing??!!!! Use the zmart bombs!!!

PILOT
Yes, sir!

As a rocket shoots off from under the helicopter, one of the Ewoks Air Scooters swings into view with CHEECH MARIN sitting in a homemade gunner's chair (like an executive's office chair that swivels has been bolted onto the futuristic air scooter that also has a shrine to the Virgin and one of those dogs with the head that bobs around.)

EWOK #3
Estan tirando los "smart bombs!"

CHEECH
I got it man, hold on, all right?

Cheech grabs a radio control and a model plane takes off the back towards the incoming rocket which tracks on the model plane and explodes.

SALVADOR
(on the back of Ewok #1's scooter)
Vaya, Compadre!!!

CUT TO:

BAD NAZI GRINGO
Fire!!!

EWOK #3
Tira!!!

(As a second missile comes in another radio control plane takes off. Same result: Rocket explodes in mid air.)

CHEECH AND EWOK #3
WHOOOOO!!!!!!

PILOT (IN HELICOPTER)
(into com mike, professional and calm)
Switching from smart bombs to laser tracking.

CO-PILOT
Roger that, we have a lock.

PILOT
Fire when ready.

CO-PILOT
Firing #3 laser guided.

EWOK #3
La Pinyata Metallica!! La Pinyata Metallica!!! Rapido, dale chico, ya!!!!

(Cheech pulls out 2 metal pinyatas shaped like donkeys with a parachutes on their backs. He throws them one after another as both Ewoks take their scooters into vertical climbs. The parachutes open. The rockets zoom towards them. Cheech pulls out a big Colt 45 revolver and shoots the pinyatas BAM! BAM! Which explode in a huge shower of metallic confetti like a rocket smoke screen, catching the two incoming rockets like Mexican Magic – BOOM! BLAM!)

PILOT
What the hell?

CO-PILOT
(a touch of awe in his voice)
It's some sort of primitive laser jamming confetti system.

PILOT
Fucking Mexican Ewoks!!!
Hit 'em with the heat seeking E-17's, see how they like that!

ROYAL NAVY

CO-PILOT
E-17's locked and loaded.

PILOT
Fire!
(Two more missiles shoot out with little red lights blinking on their nose cones)

EWOK #3
Rayos!
Dale los Chilaquiles!

CHEECH
That's my breakfast!

EWOK #3
Dale! Pronto!
(On top of the air scooter's carburetor, a cast iron pan with Chilaquiles (Mexican breakfast tortillas with eggs, rice and beans) is sizzling away. Cheech grabs the pan and throws the food out in a big arc behind the scooter.)

PILOT
Now what?

CO-PILOT
I don't know what's in that frying pan, but it's hotter 'n hell.

EWOK #3
Jalapenyos! Toma!!!

The rockets explode violently, in perhaps the most spectacular explosion yet, The fireball generated by the spicy breakfast is enormous, and it almost consumes the helicopters that have to bank radically to avoid the flames. But to the dismay of the Ewoks the helicopter makes it.

SALVADOR
Senyores osos pequenyos, no se vayan.

EWOK #3
(into com link)
Que haremos?

EWOK #1
No tenemos otro opcion.

EWOK #3
Los Globos Pianos?

EWOK #1
Los Globos.

EWOK #3
(to CHEECH)
Dale los Globos Pianos!!!

CHEECH
You sure, man?!.... OK!

Cheech opens a hatch and sets of toy balloons with smiley faces zip out the back like paratroopers coming out of a transport plane. Close Up of a piano wire spool unreeling like a fishing reel with a big fish on line.

Next shot is from the point of view of the PILOT – lines of kids balloons trailing long wires floating back towards the helicopter out the scooter.

PILOT
Now what?

BAD NAZI GRINGO
Look at zis nonszense. Kiddy balloons. How cute!
(ALL start laughing)

EXT. HELICOPTER SWOOPING AFTER THE EWOKS.

CAMERA PULLS BACK TO SHOW A CLOUD OF BALLOONS OVER THE HELICOPTERS. LAUGHTER CONTINUES.

(SUBTITLE: “Supposedly, this actually works.”)

As the helicopters fly under the cloud of balloons, the rotors suck the balloons down like vacuum fans (Close Up: the rotors from over-head as the balloons trailing wire fly down through the rotors and rap around the blades, fouling the rotor blades and tangling around them, jamming them up.)

INT. HELICOPTER:

PILOT
We're losing Power!!! (red panel lights fashing, altimeter spiraling down) May Day! May Day! White Dragon to Foxy Mama, we're going down! We are going down! OVER?!!!

EXT SHOT- HELICOPTER

Helicopter crashes in a major fireball.

EWOKS, CHEECH, SALVADOR
(as air scooter swoops out to Caribbean Sea)
WHOOOOOO! DALE!

CUT TO:

CUBAN KIDS fishing off a pier who saw the helicopter crash

CUBAN KIDS
Viste? Guau!! Mira esto! Vaya Ewoks! Vaya!!!!

CUT TO:

SALVADOR'S BIG SPEECH

EXT. – A CROSS BETWEEN A SOCCER STADIUM/ BULLFIGHT ARENA – DAY

The Mexican Ewoks and Salvador land in the center of a cheering crowd, and are escorted to a balcony or podium where Salvador is presented with a huge championship belt like the World Wrestling Federation has but encrusted with turquoise by STONE COLD STEVE AUSTIN OR SUPER-BARRIO. The podium is full of microphones like at a press conference, and a MEXICAN SPORTSCASTER is there to ask him questions like a prize fighter after a big fight:

SPORTSCASTER
Bienvenidos, campeon, bienvenidos a casa!
Welcome home, champ!

CROWD
(thousands give a huge cheer like a bull fight)
OLE!

SALVADOR
(voice booming out sound system)
Gracias, Gracias, todo el mundo!
(Thank you, thank you, everybody)

CROWD
OLE!

SPORTSCASTER
Y como tu te sientes?
(How are you feeling?)

SALVADOR
Bien, gracias a Dios, es muy bueno estar otra vez en mi campo.

CROWD
(shouts, general cheers and whistles, and a few voices yelling "welcome home!")

SPORTSCASTER
Y como fue el viaje?

SALVADOR
Pues me canse mucho. En realidad mucho mas que la pelea.

SPORTSCASTER AND OTHERS NEAR PODIUM
(laughing)
No te cansaste mucho la pelea entonces?

SALVADOR
(laughing a bit too)
Pues, eh, que puedo decir, no tanto.

SPORTSCASTER
Y entonces, pa volver a lo serio por un momento, que dijo el Presidente Crush que te enojaste tanto?

SALVADOR
Pues, no le puede decir exactamente porque hay mujeres y ninyos aqui, pero el dijo algo malo sobre mi querida mama.

CROWD (GASPS)

SPORTSCASTER
!No me digas!

SALVADOR
Pues, si, te digo.

SPORTSCASTER
Ya veo. Pero no te sientes mal porque el Presidente Crush ya es un hombre muy mayor, casi un Viejo?

SALVADOR
He pensado mucho en eso, durante mis dias en la carcel, y si es cierto. Mala mia. Pero tambien tengo manera resolverlo: Hacemos otra pelea con el hijo de la familia. Entiendo que el Gobernador Jeb Crush tiene un hijo de mas o menos 23 anyos y el sabe algo del boxeo .Tambien tengo mi hijo en Washington de la misma edad. Mi propuesto es poner los dos a boxear en Nueva York al Madison Square. ?Que piensan, ustedes?

SPORTSCASTERS/REPORTERS NEARBY/CROWD
(Murmurs, various remarks of approval and assent)

SPORTSCASTER
Interesante. Eso gana plata en pay per view, no?

OTHER REPORTERS
Demasiado! Seguro que si!

SPORTSCASTER
Pero que ganamos haciendo las peleas bobas asi?

SALVADOR
Muy buena pregunta. Sinceramente, a mi no me gusta pelear. Tuvo que irme al ejercito nacional de El Salvador de muy joven. Mate a gente. Tambien perdi a mi querida esposa, Maria Dolores en la Guerra contra los Estados Unidos. Tengo ambos experiencias de matar y perder alguien de matanza. No es bueno pelear. Pero si vamos peleando, mejor pelear de mano que de machete, no? Mejor mil veces pelear de mano que con bombas tirado de los aviones que matan ciegamente a los chicos, los abuelos, todos, cierto o no?

SPORTSCASTER AND OTHERS
Si, seguro que si, etc.

SALVADOR
La pelea de boxeo no es malo. Es saludable. Se despega el estres natural entre hombres. Pero las bombas de fuegos quimicas si son malos.

OTHER REPORTER
Pero que problema que tienes con el Presidente Crush?

SALVADOR
Este senyor es Narcotraficante y Terorista.

OTHER REPORTER
No me digas?

SALVADOR
Pues si, te digo.

OTHER REPORTER
Seguro que si?

SALVADOR
Te lo juro.

OTHER REPORTER
Pero tienes pruebas de eso?

SALVADOR
Muy buena pregunta. Si, tengo pruebas.

OTHER REPORTER
Que tipo de pruebas?

SALVADOR
Pues, algunos nosotros lo vimos los aviones en Ilopango lleno de Cocaina en aviones norteamericanos.

OTHER REPORTER
Si pero esos pueden ser otros hombres norteamericanos. Que pruebas que tienes que eses aviones pertenecen al Senyor Presidente Crush?

SALVADOR
Muy buena pregunta. Aqui tengo un amigo gringo que ha hecho un estudio muy detallada de todo los casos federales en las cortes de los Estados Unidos. Ha salido ya mucho en los periodicos y los cortes. Este estimado senyor va a darles una presentacion formal y completo
(points to Professor)
Pero para ir al grano rapidamente (whistles)
Ey, Muchachos!

(Two men in traditional Native Salvadoran clothes carry in an easel. The Professor in an expensive business suit and tie walks up to Salvador and shakes hands with him.)

SALVADOR (CONT'D)
Gracias, professor, pa' venir. (pauses) OK,...

Salvador points to Professor who turns over the blank paper

covering a picture of Crush and Manuel Noriega shaking hands.

SALVADOR (CONT'D)
Ustedes conocen al Senyor Presidente Manuel Noriega de Panama, si? Pues quien le puse este senyor Noriega en poder?

OTHER REPORTER
El Senyor Presidente Crush?

SALVADOR
Seguro que si. No era el Senyor Presidente Jimmy Carter, eh? Y por cuantos anyos eran gran amigos estes dos? Cuanto dinero La Familia Crush le dio a la Familia Noriega, saben? Y no reciben nada de vuelto? Eh, Senyores, que piensan ustedes?

(With that Salvador slaps his hands together like someone brushing the dirt off his hands after working in a field, as if to say, "OK, job well done, it's Miller Time.")

SALVADOR (CONT'D)
Entonces, estoy bien cansado del vuelo desde Cuba. Voy pa' casa a descansar y ver a la familia. Nos veremos este Sabado al juego, si?

REPORTERS
Seguro que si.

Salvador walks over to a White Horse that is waiting for him and mounts.

SALVADOR (WAVES TO CROWD)
Adios Compadres!

CROWD
OLE!
OLE!
OLE!

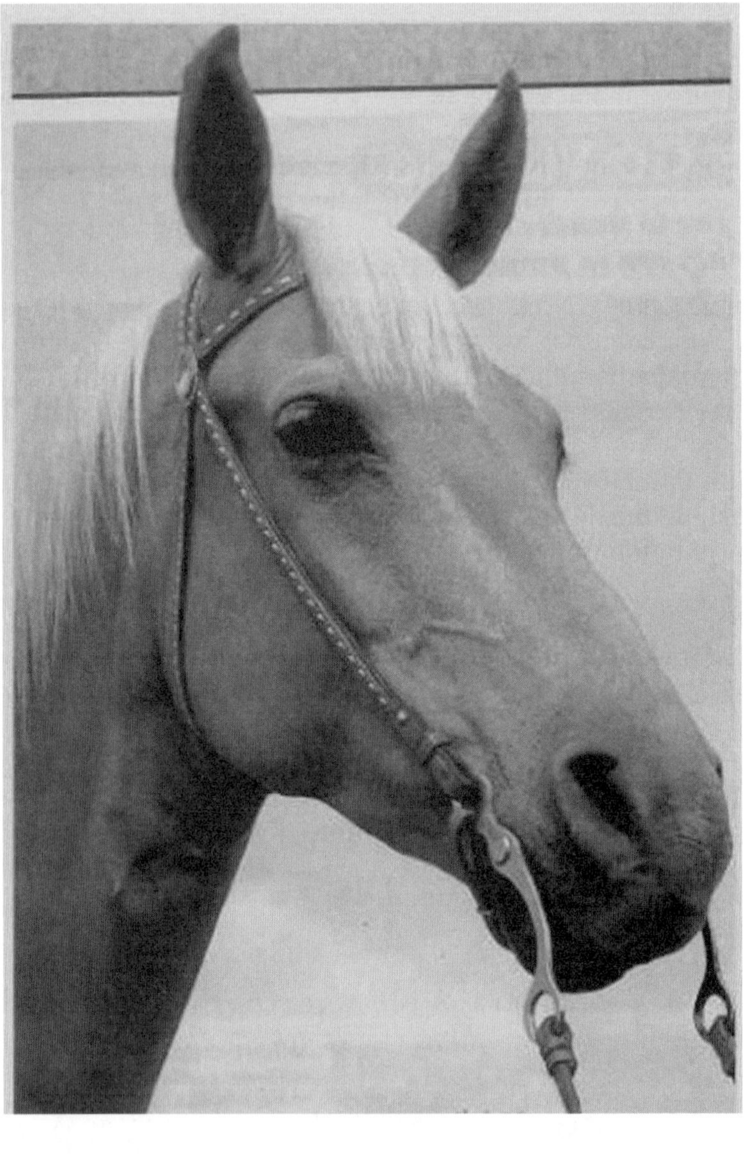

SALVADOR

(motions for microphone which is handed to him)

Y una cosita mas. Companyeros de todo el mundo. (pauses for translation which is done by MA$E appearing courtesy of Bad Boy records) Somos hermanos en el campo mundial (pause) Somos familia todos. No importa a Dios a que equipo perteneces, nunca olvides que dios nos ama a todos. Hay muchos equipos en el mundo, pero nunca olviden ustedes que nuestros hijos no pertenecen a ningun equipo – o mejor que los ninyos pertenecen al equipo universal de dios. Osea nosotros creemos en cosas politicas que no tienen sentidos por los nenes.

Tambien quiero decir, familia, que nunca quemes a la Tierra Santa. Ni tires bombas de fuego ni bombas quimicas. La Tierra es La Santa Madre. No la quemes! No importa si sea soldado o no. No la quemes!

Si queremos pelear, peleamos como hombres a Caballo, pero no se puede tirar bombas a los ninyos del aire. Es por eso que ya tenemos ninyos locos. Tirando bombas siempre pone mas debil la Madre Tierra, y la fuerza de cada ser humano viene directamente de Ella! Tirar bombas de aviones es pegar directamente a tu propio mama.

Gracias. Y adios.

(hands microphone back to reporters, waves his hat to the crowd, and rides out of the arena)

CROWD

OLE! OLE! OLE! ...OLE! OLE! OLE! ...OLE! OLE! OLE! ...
(keeps going and fades out as Salvador rides away in a cloud of dust, camera effect slowly transforms to old TV look like Cisco Kid...)

INT. – GUANTANAMO BAY PRISON CELL

Salvador wakes and looks around his nasty filthy cell. It was all just a dream.

CUT TO:

EXT - UNIVERSITY OF GUADALAJARA, MEXICO - DAY

At the beginning of the scene, the same Andean Swordsman from the titles walks by carrying his samurai sword.

ERNESTO
"Who's that?"

MANA 2
That's Chuchi.

ERNESTO
Why does he carry that big sword around?

MANA 2
Some people say that the pen is mightier than the sword, but Chuchi don't believe that way.

CUT TO:

MUSIC: JADAKISS WITH NAS - "WHY?"

A JURY OF OUR PEERS.

INT. – LA HIGH SCHOOL GYM – DAY

GARRISON KEILLER (PRAIRIE HOME COMPANION RADIO ANNOUNCER) walks to an improvised bench in the middle of the basketball court. He is relaxed and cordial as he greets people sitting in folding chairs and then sits down.

GARRISON KEILLER
Good afternoon, everybody.
(pause)
Well, I want to thank everyone for taking time out of their busy lives to come down here. I also want to thank the First Baptist Church for that fine fine meal that they just served us. Wasn't that a delicious meal? (murmurs of agreement from the crowd). Makes me wish I had brought my family, but I am

hoping to get some of you fine folk to come visit us so we can return the favor. Now I must admit I am more than a bit puzzled why I was selected to officiate here at this meeting of good folk. Some of you I know and some of you I have never met, but I was asked in all sincerity to come help out, and that is what I sincerely hope to do. This is not what I would call a festive occasion – a reason for celebration. But it is a good thing that we still have it within us to come together and talk about what ails us. The town meeting is the kind of a thing that you could see happening all over this country in days gone by. We used to have a way to get together and discuss what was troubling us – to see if we could find some sort of solution to the hard ways of the world – a world that every day seems to be more and more invasive and more and more unresponsive to the community. Used to be you knew everybody in the town you lived in. Not even that long ago, it used to be that people pretty much knew most of what and who was doing what in town. And when there was a problem, we could get together and talk about it. It wouldn't mean the problem was automatically solved, but we did have a way of actually tackling the problem ourselves. We didn't usually have a need for experts and high-priced lawyers and incomprehensible rules of evidence when we decided on a matter. Everyone who cared to come could understand pretty much every word that was said. And there wasn't all this secrecy. If you came to court, you heard what everybody else heard. We didn't have these closed sessions. We didn't spend months talking about what the jury could and couldn't hear. That was why the founding fathers decided to have a jury. So that they could decide for themselves, instead of a judge who – well - back then was working for the King of England, and – well - he was usually a pretty rich man, and so the founding fathers thought that cases should be decided by every day people instead of by big government and big money. Cause they didn't trust big government – they trusted something called democratic decisions made by non-experts and non-magistrates and non-judges. Because as we all know sometimes a government can become corrupt. That was the reason behind having a jury of your peers. Your peers – people just like you, who work the same jobs - whose kids go to the same schools - and who are not as likely to be earning a little extra money on the outcome of the case in question.

So, having said all that long winded introductory nonsense, we are gathered here today as a community, to come to grips with whether or not the government has been getting its hands dirty. It is not an easy question to answer. And we may not want to hear the answer if we somehow do manage to get to the bottom of this mess. But if it is true – and I am not here to say whether it is or not – Because that unsavory job is luckily up to the jury. But if it is true, we do need to face it. Hiding from the truth has never been any good for any country. Germany, during the 1930's hid from the truth – hoping against hope that the rumors they were hearing were not true. Or perhaps they were hoping that if they were only partly true, perhaps they were hoping that given a bit of time and faith that clearer heads would prevail. I am not trying to compare the two. I am only saying that in any given period of history, that people when dealing with the possibility of deep seated government corruption – well it is always better to know than not to know.

I think we can all agree that America has a problem with drugs. Studies show one thing very clearly. The US is the world's number one consumer of drugs, of every single kind of drug. From heroin to cocaine to marijuana, and on down the line to legal drugs like Prozac, and Vicodin, and new synthetic drugs like Crystal Methamphetamine. See, cocaine may come from Bolivia and Peru and Columbia, but they don't use it anywhere near as much as we do. We are the number one consumers of drugs in the world. Friends, the studies say that we are consuming between 70 and 90 percent of the world's drugs, and we are only 10 percent of the world's population. That is staggering when you think about it.

So we obviously do have a problem here in this country – a problem that our leaders have spent over billions of dollars in the last 30 years – money budgeted to try and reduce the amount of drugs crossing our borders. And what we are here to determine, among other things, is why has that program been such a dismal failure. Because, friends, the imports are continuing to rise. And we all know that. It's obvious as we go about our daily lives that imports are rising and rising and drug abuse in our children is going up and up. We consume between 70 and 90 percent of all the drugs in the world. I think that bears repeating.

Now a Los Angeles Police Officer has come and given testimony that he believes the US Government, instead of stopping the people trafficking in drugs has actually been helping the major drug traffickers. He says he has evidence to support that charge. He says that he has evidence that not only is the government supporting drug dealers with money and armaments, he is also saying that he has proof that the government has sold both heroin and cocaine – quantities in excess of several hundred tons. Several hundred tons of cocaine and heroin. That is just unbelievable that a government would do that kind of thing to its own citizens. None of us wants to believe that.

(pause)

But friends, we must not close our minds to the possibility. We must be willing to face the truth – no matter how ugly it may be. We must be willing to do that, because if it is true, and we ignore it – hoping it will go away – then we will have failed as the parents and guardians of the next generation. We will have failed these children who are growing up into a world where crack cocaine and crystal methamphetamine and heroin and all these pharmaceutical drugs like Vicodin, where all these drugs are becoming as commonplace in our town squares as the four basic food groups.

(pause)

So as I said this is not a joyous gathering. This is not something that truthfully I would want to be doing for the next 8 weekends. This is not even something I would have volunteered for given the option. But I was asked, and I will do my best to be responsible in discharging a duty that should have been adequately addressed by the court system back when the Christic Institute first brought it to the court's attention. I want to remind you of the words of Major Payne who said, "I am not bound by the court of King George, for he has not lived up to the measure of his own standard."

Or in the words of John Fitzgerald Kennedy, "Ask not what your country can do for you, but what you can do for your country."

(pause)

Friends, we cannot turn a blind eye to government in the question of corruption. We cannot call it patriotic to believe that our government should be allowed to do what we have gone to war to prevent other governments from doing. There is no way I will be able to justify my silence to my grand-children if this turns out to be true – if it turns out that we ignored our leaders as they brought tons of heroin and cocaine and possibly hand guns as well and caused the deaths of so many young people in this country. If these charges are true, then Mr. Crush is guilty of pushing drugs. I am not saying it is true, but the charges have been brought more than once, and they were summarily ignored several times by the courts. That is why we are forced to do the court's work. We are forced into this difficult position, but any other response would simply and plainly be cowardice.

(long pause)

So, if somebody could get me a glass of water, I seem to have gotten a bit parched making that long winded speech, lets see if we can't start this thing off, and see where it takes us. Bailiff, first witness please.

BAILIFF

(Prairie Home Companion announcer #3)

Will Mr. Michael Ruppert please take the stand.

MUSIC – CREEDENCE CLEAR WATER REVIVAL – "COME ON A RISING WIND"

FADE TO CREDITS

THE END

While credits rolling, music lowers some in volume.

EXT - MOUNTAIN LAKE IN MEXICAN MOUNTAINS - DAY

Way later in the scene with Mana by the Mountain Lake, Ruppert is there. They have him take a big bong hit, and then they go swimming and have a good time. Ruppert is awkward, but does a big corkscrew/cannonball off a rope swing and they just have a good time.

MANA

Here man, we growing this ourself man, try some.
(After wards by the pool have Ruppert meet one of the band's friends who had his arm blown off by a bomb in El Salvador. Have Ruppert take a look at it and ask him if it was White Phosphorous, and yes it was and just be quiet for a minute.)
(So then have Mana say listen mano, thank you for doing what you doing. We lost a lot of people in the war, and we need people to go to the US and explain all the costs that come from denying us our rights as human beings, so we need you to tell them what happened and how come the cocaine was used to buy the planes and the weapons they used to kill a lot of innocent people. Anyway, suerte and vaya con Dios...)
(OK so Ruppert gets out of the swimming hole and they're hanging out before getting back in their car and one of Mana comes over and pats him on the back.)

MANA1

Man it's good what you did. Don't worry now bout w'happen next, put it in God's hands and relax some OK? You doing too much work sometime. Now other people got to do what they doing too. See because nobody going to lift the earth on you shoulders man, it's too heavy. Everybody have to get together a little bit like in a party for building a house or putting the crops or anything. If everybody doing some of it, then it goes. But making the party good, is easy and also it take something different. We going to let people know what happened with this George Crush CIA thing. Then people can move together, and more work getting done that way, right?

Bernardo Gonzalez

Look, mayn, for real you gotta relax, it's OK, hiciste lo tuyo...

(see translation on p. 228-229)

RUPPERT
What does that mean? (still nervous)

MANA1
It mean relax man, you did you thing – hiciste lo tuyo – you did your thing – more nothing you can do... OK?

RUPPERT
I'll try.

MANA1
Good.

MANA2
Que pendejada dijo este?

MANA1
Que se va intentar a relajar.

MANA2
Como que what? Como que intentas a relajar?

RUPPERT
What's he saying?

MANA1
He's saying how do you trying to relax? Be like Mikie and just do it.

RUPPERT
I am Mike.

MANA1
See how easy it is?

CUT TO:

INT - TV STUDIO FOR "JEOPARDY 2112"

ALEX TREBEC is shot so full of Botox that he looks like Tom Jones about to explode in a outer space vacuum air lock, but it almost looks like at the same time he might have lost a little weight - PILATES? - you decide. The 3 contestants - Maya Angelou, the Ghost of Crazy Horse, and Tommy Chong are lined up ready for the next question.

ALEX TREBEC
All right, we are back and ready for round 2. Our categories are: "Juris Imprudence", "Shake and Bake", "Tiny Bubbles", "Pie Alamo", "Little Big Foot" and "Men and Their Flying Machines", and we turn to you Crazy Horse since I believe you won the last round.

GHOST OF CRAZY HORSE
Really? OK. Pie Alamo for three hundred, Jack.

ALEX TREBEC
And the answer is:
"This song - made famous by Camper Van Beethoven - was about a delicious dessert native to Southern Florida."

ALL THREE
(look at eachother, shrug their shoulders)
(wrong Answer Buzzer goes off)

ALEX TREBEC
"What is Key Lime Pie?" Crazy Horse, back to you.

GHOST OF CRAZY HORSE
Men and their flying machines for 500, Jack.

ALEX TREBEC
And the answer is: "This President resigned in disgrace when it was discovered that his Arbusto Energy Company's alternative energy program was actually fueled by Crack Cocaine."

GHOST OF CRAZY HORSE
All of them, Jack. Every last stinking one.
(wrong answer buzzer goes off)

ALEX TREBEC
I'm sorry that's not the answer we were looking for.

MAYA ANGELOU
(buzzes buzzer)
I have a poem entitled "The Pusher" that may be appropriate.

ALEX TREBEC
There may be time during our next commercial break, dear.

TOMMY CHONG
(buzzes buzzer) (his voice all hung over and gravelly)
I know this. Ummm. The guy with the letter. Wait - Orange Juice Crush - No, wait, I mean George Crush (he pronounces it like "Crush")

ALEX TREBEC
Let me check with the judges on that - I'm sorry - they're not allowing it. The correct pronunciation is "CROOSH" It's George Croosh, not Crush. I'm sorry - but good try.

TOMMY CHONG
Thank you, Alex

GHOST OF CRAZY HORSE
I thought he was Jack...

SPANISH TO ENGLISH TRANSLATIONS
(for the Gringos)

above
Schwarzhal
The Schwarzhal goat derives its name from its highly distinctive and attractive colour pattern. Its hindquarters are white and its forequarters black, with the dividing line at its mid-section. A herd of these uniformly marked animals make a dramatic impact in their Alpine habitat. The breed originated in the canton of Valais in Switzerland (it is also known as the Valaisanne à Col Noir, or the Walliser), but it has spread into the Rhône valley in France. It was seriously endangered at one stage, but is now making a strong comeback as a hardy, thrifty mountain goat; although its milk production is not as high as that of some of the more specialist dairy breeds of goat.

[redacted]

(Hay que esperar como siempre por el Spanglish Addiction)

Translation for pages 85-88:

MUSIC CRESCENDOS TO A RUSHING SOUND OF A JET ENGINE, THAT CHANGES SUDDENLY TO THE CRACK OF A BASEBALL BAT (MATCH ON ACTION TO SALVADOR YOU HITTING THE PLANE)
CUT TO:

HASENFUS SHOT DOWN
SCREEN TITLE: NICARAGUA OCTOBER 5TH, 1986
A field that looks very similar to the one where Young Salvador hit the home run in the opening scenes. Boys are playing baseball in the background and the kid at bat says:
Dale, ya! (do it already!)
In the distance, a cargo plane is heard and moves over center field. As all the kids turn to watch it, a kid in military fatigues comes running up. All the kids turn to him and stare. He has a shoulder mounted anti-aircraft bazooka, he lines up the sites and shoots: WHOOSH!
The planes engines start to falter and then smoke starts to pour out of it as parachutes are seen opening. PLANE CRASHES - LARGE FIREBALL

KIDS

You hitting the plane! You hitting the plane!
(match on action to Young Salvador's at bat in first scene)

INT. – NICARAGUAN LIVING ROOM – DAY
A bunch of FAT OLD MEN sit in a living room, drinking beer, watching a soccer game, and yelling at the set. Suddenly, the announcer gets on the TV. (in Spanish w/ subtitles) "We interrupt this program to bring you a special news brief" (actual news footage?)

NICARAGUAN REPORTER

We are here in Bosque del Campo where just now a US military plane was downed - officials are not sure, but it appears to be one of the narcotics trafficking missions of the secret police called the CIA. And we are here with Demetrio Macias, a boy only 15 years old, who only one hour ago, shot down the plane using only a shoulder-mounted bazooka. !What a shot, young man! How do you feel?

KID WHO SHOT DOWN HASENFUS
(Eyes shiny with happiness, surrounded by cheering fans, family, girlfriend)
I feel great, praise be to God, I always had hopes of doing something to defend the country from the invading Gringos, but I never even dreamed about something like this!!!
REPORTER
Look at this young man, and what he did with a weapon that doesn't even have radar - nothing! Impressive, no? And what do we have here? Hey Mister! Escuse me sir, what are you doing here, mayn, hey, eco-tourism? You coming to study the plant life here? What is your problem coming over here, you got no right to fly you military planes anyplace you feel, no? You getting lost in Texas and you fly 2000 miles away from you forest fire? That's what you telling me this is – a forest fire fighter plane to spray the water, right? Wh'appen mayn? My English too fast for you? You speak a some Spanish I bet no? Yes you look no so much like a forest fireman who get lost. Here you wan my cell phone so you can call them and then we can ask you Uncle what you doing flying over our country talking some story when you looking so much like a drug dealer even my grandmother can see who you is? Here take it my cell phone and call you Uncle Sam, tell him you need some lawyer, guns and money cause you get hit by a kid with a sling shot in you 20 million dollar plane OK? Here come on take it
HASENFUS
(looks dazed but takes the phone, starts dialing but can't remember all the numbers)
REPORTER
Man you no looking so good. (yells) Hey Chuchi! (whistles) Give him a little bit of water! (to Hasenfus) Here sweetheart, lemme see the phone OK?
(CU Hasenfus. Hands Reporter the phone back. From off-screen big bucket of water is thrown on him.)
HASENFUS
Hey!!! Wait whoa, hey wait, what... wha.....um .....ohhh (slumps again into daze looking off into the unfocussed distance)
REPORTER
Esweetheart, you in a bad bad shape.

###

Translation for pages 126-127

FLASHBACK: SOLDIERS KILLING TIA
EXT. RURAL EL SALVADOR – EVENING
Screen has a sort of hazy look almost out of focus - a dreamy quality. Sound is muted as well.
SUB-TITLE: "El Salvador 1984"
Soldiers in jeeps and on foot running down a hillside into a village past the town square with it's water cistern and small bandstand. They are shooting in the air - assault rifles, beating and driving people with the butts of their rifles. Animals (cows, donkeys, dogs) are running, barking, etc.
Close Up of soldiers kicking in the doors of several houses and pulling people out of the houses, and rounding them up into town square. More shots are fired. People, children are crying and screaming.
CUT TO:
INT, RURAL EL SALVADOR – CHURCH - EVENING
SALVADOR'S TIA, a nun, is trying to make a phone call to get help. You hear the line go dead. She runs accross the room to the front door, frantic, throws her body into the weight of the heavy door, and bursts outside, shouting at the soldiers.

SALVADOR'S TIA

NO! NO HAN HECHO NADA! (NO! THEY HAVEN'T DONE ANYTHING!)

A soldier she is screaming at grunts, and knocks her out with the butt of his rifle.
CUT TO:
INT -CHURCH - RURAL EL SALVADOR - DAY
SALVADOR'S TIA is on the phone yelling at the official on the other end. She is wearing nun's habit and her head is bandaged.

SALVADOR'S TIA

?But sir, where are they? The only thing I have to say is that they aren't bad people, and you can't hold people without letting us know where they are!

OFFICIAL

BuShiDo

This is a federal case. I would advise you not to get yourself into something that doesn't concern you.

SALVADOR'S TIA

Those are my neighbors! My children! How can that not concern me?!!!

###

Translation for pages 187-201

CUT TO:
GUANTANAMO --> SALVADOR CHECKS IN --> DREAM SEQUENCE.
III.2.C. SALVADOR'S ESCAPE (DREAM SEQUENCE)
INT. – GUANTANAMO BAY PRISON – DAY
We see Salvador as he is finger-printed, searched, given prison clothes, etc in rapid succession (MUSIC?). He walks into his high security cell (solitary) and goes to sleep. He wakes up the next morning, cut to him walking down the hall for breakfast . Suddenly a bomb explodes and knocks the guards down, and a group of STAR WARS EWOKS (that's right) with bands of ammo slung across their teddy bear chests come running up. Surprisingly, the little brown Ewoks speak Spanish:

EWOK #1

Let's go, man! We don't have much time!

They run down the hall, dodging occasional bullets, and jump on their Ewok air scooters, firing away, waiting for Salvador to jump on. Whooosh! They take off shooting bursts at the guard towers who are shooting at them.
Helicopters swing in behind them as they fly over and away over the Cuban Highlands. They fly through trees and canyons, with the helicopters firing away.
In one of the helicopters, a BAD NAZI GRINGO is cursing at the PILOT.

BAD NAZI GRINGO

How can you keep misszing??!!!! Use the zmart bombs!!!

PILOT

Yes, sir!

As a rocket shoots off from under the helicopter, one of the Ewoks Air Scooters swings into view with CHEECH MARIN sitting in a homemade gunner's chair (like an executive's office chair that swivels has been bolted onto the futuristic air scooter that also has a shrine to the Virgin and one of those dogs with the head that bobs around)

EWOK #3

They're firing the "smart bombs!"

CHEECH

I got it man, hold on, all right?

Cheech grabs a radio control and a model plane takes off the back towards the incoming rocket which tracks on the model plane and explodes

SALVADOR

(on the back of Ewok #1's scooter)

Go, Compadre!!!

CUT TO BAD NAZI GRINGO

Fire!!!

EWOK #3

Fire!!!

(As a second missile comes in another radio control plane takes off. Same result: Rocket explodes in mid air.)

CHEECH AND EWOK #3

WHOOOOO!!!!!!

PILOT (IN HELICOPTER)

(into com mike, professional and calm)

Switching from smart bombs to laser tracking

CO-PILOT

Roger that, we have a lock.

PILOT

Fire when ready.

CO-PILOT

Firing #3 laser guided

EWOK #3

The Metal Pinyata!!!! The Metal Pinyata!!! Quick, fire away, now!!!

Cheech pulls out 2 metal pinyatas shaped like donkeys with a parachutes on their backs. He throws them one after another as both Ewoks take their scooters into vertical climbs. The parachutes open. The rockets zoom towards them. Cheech pulls out a big Colt 45 revolver and shoots the pinyatas BAM!

BAM! Which explode in a huge shower of metallic confetti like a rocket smoke screen, catching the two incoming rockets like Mexican Magic – BOOM! BLAM!

PILOT

What the hell?

CO-PILOT

(a touch of awe in his voice)

It's some sort of primitive laser jamming confetti system.

PILOT

Fucking Mexican Ewoks!!!

Hit 'em with the heat seeking E-17's, see how they like that!

CO-PILOT

E-17's locked and loaded

PILOT

Fire!

(Two more missiles shoot out with little red lights blinking on their nose cones)

EWOK #3

Shit!

Give 'em the Chilaquiles!

CHEECH

That's my breakfast!

EWOK #3

Do it!!! NOW!!!

(On top of the air scooter's carburetor, a cast iron pan with Chilaquiles (Mexican breakfast tortillas with eggs, rice and beans) is sizzling away. Cheech grabs the pan and throws the food out in a big arc behind the scooter.)

PILOT

Now what?

CO-PILOT

I don't know what's in that frying pan, but it's hotter 'n hell.

EWOK #3

Jalapenyos! Take that!!!

The rockets explode violently, in perhaps the most spectacular explosion yet, The fireball generated by the spicy breakfast is enormous, and it almost consumes the helicopters that have to bank radically to avoid the flames. But to the dismay of the Ewoks the helicopter makes it.

SALVADOR
Mister Little Bears, they're still following us.
EWOK #3
(into com link)
What do we do?
EWOK #1
We have no other option.
EWOK #3
The Piano Balloons?
EWOK #1
The Balloons.
EWOK #3
(to CHEECH)
Give 'em the Piano Balloons!!!
CHEECH
You sure, man?! OK!

Cheech opens a hatch and sets of toy balloons with smiley faces zip out the back like paratroopers coming out of a transport plane. Close Up of a piano wire spool unreeling like a fishing reel with a big fish on line. Next shot is from the point of view of the PILOT – lines of kids balloons trailing long wires floating back towards the helicopter out the scooter.

PILOT
Now what?
BAD NAZI GRINGO
Look at zis nonszense. Kiddy balloons. How Cute!
(ALL start laughing)

EXT. HELICOPTER SWOOPING AFTER THE EWOKS. CAMERA PULLS BACK TO SHOW A CLOUD OF BALLOONS OVER THE HELICOPTERS. LAUGHTER CONTINUES.
(SUBTITLE: "Supposedly, this actually works.")
As the helicopters fly under the cloud of balloons, the rotors suck the balloons down like vacuum fans (CU: the rotors from over-head as the balloons trailing wire fly down through the rotors and rap around the blades, fouling the rotor blades and tangling around them, jamming them up.
INT. HELICOPTER:

PILOT
We're losing Power!!! (red panel lights fashing, altimeter

spiraling down) May Day! May Day! White Dragon to Foxy Mama, we're going down! We are going down! OVER?!!!

EXT SHOT- HELICOPTER

Helicopter crashes in a major fireball

EWOKS, CHEECH, SALVADOR

(as air scooter swoops out to Caribbean Sea)

WHOOOOOO! GOT 'EM!

CUT TO: CUBAN KIDS FISHING OFF A PIER WHO SAW THE HELICOPTER CRASH

CUBAN KIDS

You saw that? Wow! Look at that! Go, Ewoks, GO!!!

SALVADOR'S BIG SPEECH

EXT. – A CROSS BETWEEN A SOCCER STADIUM/ BULLFIGHT ARENA – DAY

The Mexican Ewoks and Salvador land in the center of a cheering crowd, and are escorted to a balcony or podium where Salvador is presented with a huge championship belt like in the World Wrestling Federation has but encrusted with turquoise by STONE COLD STEVE AUSTIN OR SUPER-BARRIO. The podium is full of microphones like at a press conference, and a MEXICAN SPORTSCASTER is there to ask him questions similar to a prize fighter after a big fight:

SPORTSCASTER

Bienvenidos, campeon, bienvenidos a casa!

(Welcome home, champ!)

CROWD

(thousands give a huge cheer like a bull fight)

OLE!

SALVADOR

(voice booming out sound system)

Gracias, Gracias, todo el mundo!

(Thank you, thank you, everybody)

CROWD

OLE!

SPORTSCASTER

Y como tu te sientes?

(How are you feeling?)

SALVADOR

Good, thank God, it's very good to be home again.
CROWD
(shouts general cheers and whistles and a few voices yelling welcome home!)
SPORTSCASTER
And how was the trip?
SALVADOR
Well, it was tiring. In reality much more than the fight.
SPORTSCASTER AND OTHERS NEAR PODIUM
(laughing)
The fight wasn't that tiring, then?
SALVADOR
(laughing a bit too)
Well, what can I say - not that much.
SPORTSCASTER
And so, to return to serious matters for a minute, what did President Crush say that got you so mad?
SALVADOR
I can't say exactly, because there are women and children here, but he said something bad about my dear mother.
CROWD (GASPS)
SPORTSCASTER
!NO WAY!
SALVADOR
Way.
SPORTSCASTER
I see. But don't you feel bad, because President Crush is an older man, almost a Grandfather?
SALVADOR
I have thought a lot about this during my days in prison, and it is true. My bad. But I also have come up with a way to resolve that problem. Let's make another fight with the son of the family. I understand that Governor Jeb Crush has a son who's about 23 years old and that he knows something about boxing. I also have a son in Washington about the same age. I propose that we have the fight in New York at Madison Square Garden. What do you gentlemen think of that?
SPORTSCASTERS/REPORTERS NEARBY/CROWD
(Murmurs, various remarks of approval and assent)

SPORTSCASTER

Interesting. That would make money on pay per view, right?

OTHER REPORTERS

A lot of money! No doubt!

SPORTSCASTER

But what do we gain with stupid fights like these?

SALVADOR

Very good question. Sincerely, I don't like to fight. I had to go to El Salvador's National Army when I was very young. I killed people. I also lost my beloved wife, Maria Dolores, in the war with the United States. I know what it is to kill and to have someone you love die. It is no good fighting. But if we have to fight, it is better to fight with your bare hands than with a machete, no? A thousand times better to fight with your hands than with bombs thrown out of planes that blindly kill children, old people, anyone, true or not?

SPORTSCASTER AND OTHERS

Yes, Of course, etc.

SALVADOR

Boxing is not bad. It's healthy. It relieves the natural stress between men. But chemical firebombs - those are bad

OTHER REPORTER

But what problem do you have with President Crush?

SALVADOR

The man is a Drug Dealer and a Terrorist.

OTHER REPORTER

No way!

SALVADOR

Way.

OTHER REPORTER

Are you sure?

SALVADOR

I swear.

OTHER REPORTER

But you have proof of this?

SALVADOR

Very good question. Yes, I have proof.

OTHER REPORTER

What kind of proof?

SALVADOR

Well, some of us saw the airplanes at Ilopango full of Cocaine - and they were North American planes

OTHER REPORTER

Yes, but they could have belonged to other men in North America. What proof do you have that these planes belonged to President Crush?

SALVADOR

Very good question. I brought with me a Gringo friend of mine that has made a detailed study of all the federal cases in the North American federal courts. He has appeared in many newspapers and courts. This esteemed man is going to give you a complete formal presentation (points to Professor who is standing on side of stage) But.. to get to the heart of the matter a little faster (whistles) Hey, muchachos!

(Two men in typical Salvadoran clothes carry in an easel. The Professor in an expensive business suit and tie walks up to Salvador and shakes hands with him.)

SALVADOR (CONT'D)

Thank you, Professor, for coming (pauses) OK,

Salvador points to Professor who turns over the blank paper covering a picture of President George Crush and President Manuel Noriega shaking hands.

SALVADOR (CONT'D)

You all know the President of Panama, Manuel Noriega, yes? Well, who put this man Noriega in power?

OTHER REPORTER

President Crush?

SALVADOR

That's right. It wasn't President Jimmy Carter, was it? And for how many years were they good friends, these two? How much money did the Crush Family give to the Noriega Family, do you know? And they didn't get anything in return for all that money? Gentlemen, what do you think?

(With that Salvador slaps his hands together like someone brushing the dirt off his hands after working in a field, as if to say, OK job well done, it's Miller Time.)

So, I am pretty tired after the flight from Cuba. I am going home to rest and see my family. See you guys at the game on

Saturday, OK?
REPORTERS
Sure thing, champ.
Salvador walks over to a White Horse that is waiting for him and mounts
SALVADOR (TO CROWD)
Good-bye Compadres!
CROWD
OLE!
SALVADOR
(motions for microphone which is handed to him)
And one more thing. Friends from all over the world. (pauses for translation which is done by MA$E, appearing courtesy of Bad Boy Records) We are brothers in this worldwide playing field. We are all family. It doesn't matter to God what team you belong to, never forget that God loves all of us. There are many teams in the world, but never forget that our children don't belong to any team - or maybe better the children belong to the universal team of God. Meaning that we believe in Political things that don't make any sense to children
I also want to say, family, never burn the Mother Earth. Never throw fire-bombs or chemical bombs. The Earth is the Holy Mother. Don't burn her! It doesn't matter if you are a soldier or not. Don't burn her! If you want to fight, then fight like men - on horseback, but you cannot throw bombs on the children from the air. That's why the children are crazy now. Throwing bombs always makes Mother Earth weaker, and the strength of each heman being comes directly from Her!!! Throwing bombs from planes is like hitting your own mother. Thank you. A Dios!.
(hands microphone back to reporters, waves his hat to the crowd, and rides out of the arena)
CROWD
OLE! OLE! OLE! (keeps going and fades out as Salvador rides away in a cloud of dust, camera effect slowly transforms to old TV look like Cisco Kid)

INT. – GUANTANAMO BAY PRISON CELL
Salvador wakes and looks around his nasty filthy cell. It was all

just a dream.
###

Translation for pages 209-210

WHILE CREDITS ROLLING

Way later in the scene with Mana by the Mountain Lake have Ruppert there and have them make him take a big bong hit and then they go swimming and have a good time. Ruppert is awkward but does a big corkscrew/cannonball off a rope swing and they just have a good time

MANA

Here man, we growing this ourself man, try some

Then after wards or by the pool have Ruppert meet one of the band's friends who had his arm blown off by a bomb in El Salvador. Have Ruppert take a look at it and ask him if it was White Phosphorous and yes it was and just be quiet for a minute.

So then have Mana say listen mano, thank you for doing what you doing. We lost a lot of people in the war, and we need people to go to the US and explain all the costs that come from denying us our rights as human beings, so we need you to tell them what happened and how come the cocaine was used to buy the planes and the weapons they used to kill a lot of innocent people. Anyway, suerte and vaya con Dios...

OK so Ruppert gets out of the swimming hole and they're hanging out before getting back in their car and one of Mana comes over and pats him on the back

MANA1

Man it's good what you did. Don't worry now bout w'happen next, put it in God's hands and relax some OK? You doing too much work sometime. Now other people got to do what they doing too. See because nobody going to lift the earth on you shoulders man, it's too heavy. Everybody have to get together a little bit like in a party for building a house or putting the crops or anything. If everybody doing some of it, then it goes. But making the party good, is easy and also it take something different. We going to let people know what happened with

this George Crush CIA thing. Then people can move together, and more work getting done that way, right?
Look, mayn, for real you gotta relax, it's OK, hiciste lo tuyo...

RUPPERT

What does that mean? (still nervous)

MANA1

It mean relax man, you did you thing – hiciste lo tuyo – you did your thing – more nothing you can do... OK?

RUPPERT

I'll try.

MANA1

Good.

MANA2

What stupid thing did he say?

MANA1

That he's gonna try and relax.

MANA2

That what? How do you make an attempt to relax?

RUPPERT

What's he saying?

MANA1

He's saying how do you trying to relax? Be like Mikie and just do it.

RUPPERT

I am Mike.

MANA1

See how easy it is?

MORE CREDITS

Other books you want to read if you want to know:

El Senyor Presidente by Miguel "Mike" Asturias

Cocaine Politics by Peter Dale Scott

The Politics of Heroin by Alfred W. McCoy

Dark Alliance by Gary Webb

The Black Jacobins (Toussaint and Boukman and a place called Cannes Brulees) by Jack "Creole" Carney

Mexican Newspapers – Google it, pendejo, or even go to a library already so you can be more anonymous and clandestino like Manu Chau and shit... bODEGAS gOT 'eM 2, ...but don't use your card, or the Man will know, and it will go on your permanent record that you speak a subversive language (Mexican). (The King wants to play...)

Life and Times of Earl "The Goat" Manigault by Various Artists/United Artists moving **PICTURES**

Bird – The Making of An American Sports Legend by Lee Daniel Levine.

The Sniper by Liam O'Flaherty

Los de Abajo (The Under-Dogs) by Mariano Azuela

The Invisible Man by Ralph Ellison

Monkey - Folk Novel of China by Wu Ch'eng-En

Big Daddy Kane by Kool DJ The Red Alert Y'all

ORIGINAL OR COPY????

About the Author

Bernardo Gonzolez migrates

If you give him a dollar, he'll tell you a story
Kind of like Dr. Doolittle.
If you give him a few dollars, and he likes you,
he'll fix your plumbing.
Kind of like Robert DeNiro in Brazil.
He can dance to Indonesian mystical music,
and can to make a pretty good fountain.
(try it some time)
If he gives you his word, he makes good on it.